"I thought Jackson was bringing home a girl," Tabitha says.

"I think we all just assumed it," Momma said, sitting back down at the breakfast table. "I guess not."

Tabitha glances over at me. I'm keeping my gaze focused on the tea in my mug.

"He's kinda cute," she says in what is obviously intended as a little whisper.

"I hadn't noticed," I say.

I almost miss the glance exchanged between Momma and Tabitha before they go back to talking about cribs and high chairs.

Anyone with any sense at all would know that I was lying. Anybody who took one look at Daniel could see that he was not only kinda cute, he was drop dead gorgeous.

The kind of handsome man that no doubt had women falling at his feet.

And with that slow grin of his, he obviously knows it.

There is nothing more dangerous to a woman's heart than a handsome pilot in uniform.

Coming from a family of pilots AND working with pilots every day, I've been inoculated.

Handsome pilots don't have an effect on me.
Until they do.

Finding True North

ALPINE FALLS

KATHRYN KALEIGH

FINDING TRUE NORTH
PREVIEW — *A GHOST OF CHRISTMAS MAGIC*

Copyright © by Kathryn Kaleigh

Written by Kathryn Kaleigh.
Published by KST Publishing
Cover by Skyhouse24Media
www.kathrynkaleigh.com

Christmas in Alpine Falls

(Reading Order)

Stranded in Alpine Falls

Belonging in Alpine Falls

The Spirit of Christmas in Alpine Falls

Christmas Wishes in Alpine Falls

Finding True North in Alpine Falls

A Ghost of Christmas Magic in Alpine Falls

All of the books in the Alpine Falls Series standalone and can be read out of order. However, some books have characters from the previous stories in them.

Contemporary

(Reading Order by series)

(VOWS OF INHERITANCE SERIES)

Vow to Protect

Vow to Redeem

(ALPINE FALLS SERIES)

Secrets and Second Chances

Honeymoon with a Stranger

Not Our Wedding

Stranded in Alpine Falls

Belonging in Alpine Falls

The Spirit of Christmas in Alpine Falls

Christmas Wishes in Alpine Falls

Finding True North in Alpine Falls

A Ghost of Christmas Magic in Alpine Falls

(SILVER PINES SERIES)

The Way Back to You

Back to Where We Began

When We Were Us

(ONCE UPON FOREVER SERIES)

My Forever Guy

Our Forever Love

Forever Vows

Finding Forever

Accidentally Forever

(TRUE NORTH SERIES)

Borrowed Until Monday

Still Mine

The Moon and the Stars at Christmas

Perfectly Mismatched

On the Way to Forever

A Merry Little Christmas

On the Way Home to Christmas

It was Always You

(UNBREAK MY HEART SERIES)

Begin Again

Love Again

Falling Again

(FOR THE LOVE OF THE FLIGHT SERIES)

Just Stay

Just Chance

Just Believe

Just Us

Just Once

Just Happened

Just Maybe

Just Pretend

Just Because

(MAGNETIC NORTH SERIES)

Second Chance Kisses

Second Chance Secrets

First Time Charm

Three Broken Rules

Second Chance Destiny

Unexpected Vows

(FALLING FOR CHRISTMAS SERIES)

The Heart of Christmas

The Magic of Christmas

In a One Horse Open Sleigh

A Secret Royal Christmas

An Old Fashioned Christmas

(CITY SKYLINE BILLIONAIRES SERIES)

Billionaire's Unexpected Landing

Billionaire's Accidental Girlfriend

Billionaire's Fallen Angel

Billionaire's Secret Crush

Billionaire's Barefoot Bride

(TRULY, MADLY, DEEPLY SERIES)

The Lady in the Red Dress

On the Edge of Chance

Sealed with a Kiss

Kiss Me at Midnight

The Heart Knows

(STOLEN ECHOES SERIES)

When Cupid's Arrow Strikes

Chasing Fireflies

A Chance Encounter

(EDGE OF THE HORIZON SERIES)

The Forever Equation

Pretend Boyfriend

All our Tomorrows

Kissing for Keeps

Out of the Blue

The Princess and the Playboy

(RED LIPSTICK KISSES SERIES)

Red Lipstick Kisses and Small Town Wishes

Stolen Dances and Big City Chances

Chance Connections and Upside Down Plans

A Christmas Kiss on the Twenty-Fifth

Believe in the Magic of Christmas

All of the books in each Series are standalone and can be read out of order. However, some books have characters from the previous stories in them.

ROMANTASY

(IN THE SPIRIT OF LOVE)
Spirits of the Heart

Out of Dreams and Ashes

Etched Upon the Heart

WESTERN ROMANCE

(LONE STAR HEARTS)
Wanted by a Texas Ranger

Saved by a Texas Ranger

(WHISKEY SPRINGS)
Finding Natalie

Promising Samantha

Falling for Allyson

Saving Savannah

Claiming Charlie

Rescuing Keira

Protecting Gabriella

Courting Isabella

TIME TRAVEL

(INTO THE MIST)
Written in the Wind

Scripted in the Stars

Destined in the Twilight

Promised in the Mist

Trapped in the Melody

(DRAGON'S BLOOD)

Dragon's Blood

Lavender Blue

Champagne Silver

Twilight Frost

Mountbatten Pink

(WHEN HEARTSTRINGS BECKON)

Rescued in Time

Meet me in 1879

(WHEN HEARTSTRINGS ECHO)

Messages Across Time

Falling Through to Forever

Once Upon a Winter's Spell

(BECKONED)

Before the Storm

Twist of Fate

When the Stars Align

Once Upon a Christmas

Once in a Blue Moon

A Wish Upon a Star

(BEGUILED)

When Lightning Strikes

Storm of Time

Midnight Storm

When the Moon Falls

Stormborn Angel

(SPELLED)

Time Tempest

The Heart Remembers

A Moment in Time

Moonlight Shadows

HISTORICAL

(TAPESTRY OF BLUE AND GRAY)

Shadows Beneath Magnolia Blooms

Secrets Among Southern Roses

(IT HAPPENED BY ACCIDENT)

Accidentally Alluring

Accidentally Married

(SOUTHERN BELLE CIVIL WAR)

Beyond Enemy Lines

Love Always

Hearts Under Siege

Hearts Under Fire

Away Down South in Dixie

The Reluctant Bride

Stay with Me

Jasmine Kisses

Magnolia Kisses

Gardenia Kisses

(THE QUINNS)

Wait for Me

Take Me Home

Keep Me Safe

FATED MATES

Riley's Mate

Aiden's Mate

Brayden's Mate

STANDALONE SUSPENSE

Lost and Found

All I Want for Christmas

Serenity

Courting Alley Cat

The best and most beautiful things in the world cannot be seen nor even touched, but just felt in the heart.

-Helen Keller 1891

Finding True North

Chapter One

Andrea Flynn
December

SEATBELT. CHECK.

Landing gear down. Check.

Flaps down. Check.

Final approach to the Alpine Falls runway.

My first trip home flying solo.

The last time I came home, my brother Christopher had flown me here in his helicopter. It hadn't been a big deal. Just a run-of-the-mill trip he made all the time.

Not like this one.

The snowcapped mountain peaks on three sides of the vale stand tall and jagged.

The runway below looks like a postage stamp from my vantage point.

Nothing at all like the complex runways I'm accustomed to navigating.

Flying at this elevation is somewhat different from flying at lower elevations.

I keep my eyes on the computer monitors. Watching wind speed. Crosswinds.

Fortunately, it's a clear day. Nothing out of the ordinary.

Alpine Falls comes in right at ten thousand feet in elevation.

An extraordinarily high elevation for a town. And yet everyone who lives here calls the snowcapped mountains surrounding it on three sides the high country.

It typically snows here before Christmas in Alpine Falls, probably about fifty percent of the time. Maybe seventy percent.

The runway is a little tiny postage stamp surrounded by trees on all sides. A rushing mountain stream on one side. On the other side is a packed earth trail leading to the Alpine Lodge and my family's home.

The trees, maple, aspen, and pine, have all shed their leaves since the last time I was here, but the blue spruce trees still have their needles. The blue spruce trees look like a grove of undecorated Christmas trees, which I suppose in some ways, they really are.

This is apparently one of those years when the snow doesn't fall before Christmas. I see no signs of snow on the ground as I take the little Cessna in for a landing.

This isn't one of the usual airplanes I fly. In fact, it isn't even a Skye Travels airplane. It's one of my boss's private planes that he'd generously allowed me to borrow for the week.

Those few seconds of ground effect before the airplane wheels hit the runway are the one time when the airplane actually feels like it's floating. Maybe it's just me.

Probably just me since technically it's floating the whole time it's in the air.

My wheels bump against the runway and the plane slows to a stop. I taxi around to one of the areas designated for parking. There is no terminal. No building at all. The runway has nothing more than two air socks. Three would be better for crosswind detection.

I proceed to go through the usual post-flight checklist.

I check my watch. I've landed thirty minutes earlier than I had anticipated.

Not that I expect a lot of fanfare for my first solo flight home. However. With five brothers and sisters, four of them married, it seems a bit to me like someone would have shown up to meet me and to witness my first landing at the Alpine Falls runway. Such that it is.

Literally just a runway.

There's no one here.

But I'm early.

I secure the airplane and open the door.

The cold wind, even though I grew up with it, catches me off-guard as it slaps me in the face.

I grab my coat on the seat next to me and shrug into it,

buttoning it up. I didn't bring gloves or a hat, but we always have extra at the house.

With my coat on now, I climb out of the airplane and open up the cargo area.

Unlike my sisters, I have learned to travel light. I'm home for a week with just one small suitcase.

I double-check to make sure I have everything. My phone case strapped over my shoulders. The airplane locked. My luggage.

With everything I need, I start down the path leading home.

Even though I currently live in Denver, Alpine Falls will always be the place I think of as home.

Being the youngest of six siblings, three of whom still live in Alpine Falls along with our parents, there is always someone in the family around.

Unless, of course, I'm wanting to show off my landing skills.

The air is a lot lighter than I'm used to and I can feel my skin drying out already.

I'm prepared. I have lots of moisturizer in my luggage. That's something I never forget.

Dragging my suitcase behind me, I turn left at a fork in the path. The path to the right leads to the Alpine Lodge. My family owns the lodge and my oldest sister, Arabella, runs it as the official manager. But it's a family business and everyone chips in when they're around. I'll be given some task or another, too, while I'm here. I don't mind. It's expected. We all grew up working at the lodge.

I'm especially looking forward to seeing my brother Jackson. Jackson, like me, is a private pilot.

And Jackson, like me, works for Skye Travels. I work in Denver, though, and he works in the Houston office.

I still have hope that we'll someday at least work in the same city, but that would probably require me to move to Houston.

The Skye Travels home office is based in Houston where it was started by Noah Worthington and that's where most of the company's airplanes are housed.

Noah founded Skye Travels with just one little Cessna airplane and a whole lot of legendary customer service.

Now he owns and operates the largest private airline company in the country. Like Alpine Lodge, Skye Travels is family owned and operated. So much so that all things being equal, he'll hire his family first. To his credit, even though he boldly embraces nepotism, he makes sure that anyone he hires, especially his family, even more so, is the most qualified person for the job.

My brother and I were lucky to get hired on with Skye Travels. The competition is steep.

A little chipmunk runs up in front of me, stands on his hind legs, then realizing I'm not going to feed him, takes off just as fast.

The chipmunks always make me smile.

I follow the path to the back door of the house and walk in through the unlocked door.

I roll my eyes. This would never happen on purpose in Denver. After living away from Alpine Falls, first for college, then for work, I don't think I can ever go back to feeling comfortable leaving my door unlocked.

Too much can happen.

And the lodge is just a quick walk away. More people means more opportunities to have someone wander in.

I automatically take off my coat and hang it on one of pegs near the back door before going into the kitchen.

Tabitha, sitting at the breakfast table, looks up. Tabitha is my oldest brother's wife. Moose, her big solid white husky stands up and wags his tail.

"Andrea," she says with a glance at her watch. "You're early."

Tabitha has Christmas wrapping paper, ribbons, and boxes spread all over the table.

"A little," I say, pleased that someone at least noticed that I was early. I run my hands over Moose's head and he licks me affectionately.

"I was planning on walking down to meet you at the airport."

Tabitha, bless her heart, was still calling the runway an airport.

"It's okay."

She stands up and puts both hands on her very huge, very pregnant stomach and stretches her back.

"How are you feeling?" I ask. She can't possibly be feeling like walking anywhere.

"I feel good," she says, smiling. "I'm big as a house, huh?"

She must have seen my shocked expression. I force myself to smile back.

"A little bigger than the last time I saw you." I glance around. "Where is everybody else?" Surely she didn't need to be here alone.

"Here and there. Your mother is upstairs getting the guest room ready."

"Guest room?" Most guests took rooms over at the lodge. That's what it was for after all. Only special friends of the family stayed in one of our guest rooms here at our house.

"Jackson's bringing a friend home for the week."

"Oh." I'd been looking forward to catching up with Jackson, but if he was bringing a girlfriend, then I could forget spending any quality time with him.

I obviously hadn't brought a boyfriend. It had been about six months since I'd even gone out with anyone and from the looks of what was available out there in the dating world, I was better off by far being single.

"Can I get you anything before I take my things upstairs?"

Tabitha bites her lip. "I was going to ask if I could get you anything."

I've always liked Tabitha. She has a huge heart and a generous spirit.

"Let me get settled in and I'll come back down for some hot tea. You can drink tea, right?"

Tabitha grins. "Sure can. I'll get everything ready."

Knowing I'm fighting a losing battle on keeping her from doing anything for me, I agree and head upstairs to my room.

The big house rambles. That's the best way to describe it. I walk through the foyer, past the old grandfather clock that punctuates the minutes and head upstairs.

The house started out as what most people would call a normal house. But now, even though it has eight bedrooms and nine bathrooms on three different floors, there is never any crowded feeling. Not even when we're all here together.

Technically, it isn't just a house. It's what most people called a mansion. I personally call it a manor, even though everyone tends to think that title a bit too European.

The nearby lodge, Alpine Lodge, had actually been built before the house. The lodge has been in the family since my great-great grandparents claimed the land and proceeded to grow their family of twelve children.

After their children (nine daughters) left home, they had begun renting out the many vacant rooms. That was how the lodge was born.

Their son, my great grandfather had married and together he and his wife had built the house that my family now lives in. They, too, had a large family and although they had started off with a normal sized house, each generation built on more rooms over the years. Each generation, it seemed, added one touch or another to the house. The effect was a large rambling house with plenty of room for extended family.

Even when I had lived here with two married brothers and one married sister, we all never stepped on each other's toes. It was only after people visited our house that they understood how adult children could live with their parents and it not be weird.

Our parents had their own two-story suite of rooms and their own entrance to the outside.

The house was that big and rambling.

The kitchen was one part of the house that we all shared. The kitchen, breakfast room, and the dining room.

My room, on the second floor, still carries a vibe from my teenage years. I took down all the rock star posters before I left home, but my trophies and books still fill a bookcase along one wall.

I open up my suitcase and quickly hang my clothes in the closet. As a pilot, I learned to travel with all my clothes on hangers. Saves countless time and energy.

I change out of my pilot's uniform into a pair of jeans and a gray Alpine Falls sweatshirt.

After washing my face and giving my hair a quick brushing, I pull it back in a messy ponytail. Good enough.

After Jackson gets here, I'll probably go over to the lodge. Check out the Christmas decorations. My sister, Arabella will doubtlessly put me to work, but I'll take the book I'm reading with me just in case I have time to relax in front of the big stone fireplace.

Leaving my room, I see my mother coming from the guest room down the hall.

"There's my favorite daughter," she says, pulling me into a big hug.

Of course I know I'm not her favorite daughter. She tells all of us that. Besides, we all know that Christopher, the oldest, is her favorite child.

It became especially obvious when she talked Daddy into building a helipad near the runway in order to lure him back to Alpine Falls. How could we not notice?

"I heard Jackson is bringing a friend home," I say as we walk side by side toward the stairs. "Have we met her before?"

"I didn't even ask," Mama says. "He just asked if the guest room was available." She glances over at me with a sideways glance. "I should have asked you if you were bringing anyone."

"I would have told you," I say, biting back a sigh. "but no. Not this year."

"You know," she says, locking an arm with mine. "You're not getting any younger."

"Momma." I roll my eyes. "You've got Tabitha just about ready to pop. You shouldn't be worried about me getting married."

"Just because you're the youngest doesn't mean you shouldn't be thinking about getting married and settling down."

I take a deep breath. "I will take that opinion under advisement," I say. "But it's not like it was when you were growing up. People, especially career people, wait until they're in their thirties to get married."

Now Momma rolls her eyes.

"You have no idea how quickly time flies. Just don't wait too long."

"Yes. Momma."

"You and Jackson might as well be twins."

"You're so very lucky to have two of us."

As we walk down the stairs, I wonder what's come over my mother. She hardly ever gives me a hard time about settling down.

Probably something in the air.

Maybe it has something to do with it being Christmas.

Christmas puts everyone in a different kind of mood.

As for me, I had no intention of settling down anytime soon and I had every intent of spending this Christmas without the complications of a boyfriend.

Chapter Two

Daniel Worthington

IT'S MY FIRST TIME TO THE LITTLE TOWN OF ALPINE Falls.

"Prepare for landing," Jackson Flynn says into the headset.

Habit. It's just habit. We're the only two in the airplane. Jackson is in the pilot's seat and I'm in the copilot's seat.

I look out the window at the little town unfolding below. It's more like a community, really, than a town. Born and raised in Houston, I'm a big city guy. Nonetheless, I've flown into my share of small towns.

Jackson takes the plane down toward the runway.

The familiar sound of the wheels going down. The flaps down. The chatter from the nearby Glenwood Springs airport.

Jackson and I both work as pilots for Skye Travels. Hired at the same time, we'd bonded during orientation three years ago.

"Are you sure your family won't mind me intruding on their Christmas?"

"I promise it's not an intrusion. We're a big family. I doubt they'll even notice you're here."

"I'm going to take that in the best possible way," I say.

"As you should."

My parents had decided to jet off to Switzerland for Christmas this year to celebrate their recent retirement. They were calling it a second honeymoon. I think that was their way of not inviting me.

As such I hadn't made any plans for Christmas. It wasn't a big deal if I ended up spending it alone. I wasn't a scrooge, but being an only child, I was used to quiet holidays.

Jackson, however, wouldn't have it. He insisted on me joining his family in Alpine Falls.

I had to admit I was curious. I'd never spent Christmas in a small town or with a large family. It promised to be an interesting week.

Our wheels touch the runway and I notice another airplane already parked. As to be expected in a small town, there is no terminal. Just a couple of air socks.

"Someone's already here," I say as he taxies over to park next to the little Cessna.

"I don't recognize that airplane," Jackson says.

"It's not one of ours," I say, stating the obvious since there is no Skye Travels logo splashed across it. "Probably belongs to a guest."

"Probably." A quick Internet search of Alpine Lodge had told me it was an old, but elegant lodge. A Christmas destination for many.

Apparently people come here year after year to spend their Christmas holiday at the lodge.

My phone chimes with a text message.

"Anything important?" Jackson asked.

"Sophia."

"I thought you two broke up."

I thought so, too," I say, putting my phone away without reading the message.

"Hasn't snowed yet," Jackson says as he goes through the post flight checklist.

"Is that unusual?"

He shrugs. "Somewhat." He glances toward the rugged mountain peaks with white clouds clustering around them. "It'll snow sometime this week."

Snow wasn't in the forecast, but since Jackson had grown up here, I'd take his forecast over the meteorologists' any day.

"I hope so," I say. "A white Christmas will be a new experience."

"I feel sorry for you," Jackson says.

"Do we have transportation coming?" I ask, changing the subject.

"We walk," Jackson says.

I raise an eyebrow. This is most definitely going to be a

different experience. Different from any other Christmas I've ever had.

A Christmas to remember.

We put on our coats, climb out of the airplane, and pull our suitcases out of the cargo hold.

Jackson had not been kidding. Our transportation consisted of walking.

Rolling our suitcases behind us, we follow the packed dirt trail from the runway into the trees.

"It's pretty here," I say as we walk through a grove of blue spruce trees.

"You should see it in the fall before the maple and aspen trees shed their leaves."

"I can imagine. I haven't spent much time in this part of the country."

"It gets into your blood," Jackson says.

We turn left at a fork in the path.

"Go that way," Jackson says. "to get to the lodge. Then keep going to get to town."

"Got it." I pull my collar up over my ears to keep the bitingly cold wind from killing my ears.

We go in through the back door of what looks like a big rambling house. An old house, but well maintained.

Three women sit at the kitchen table drinking from coffee cups.

"There's my favorite son," the older woman pulls Jackson into a hug.

"She says that to all of us," Jackson says. "This is my mother." He turns to the other women. "My very pregnant sister-in-law, Tabitha, and my sister."

"It's a pleasure to meet you Mrs. Flynn," I say. "I've heard nothing but good things about you.

My gaze touches his sister-in-law, then slides to his sister and freezes.

Chapter Three

Andrea

I BREATHE IN THE STEAM WAFTING OUT OF THE MUG of hot tea, then take a little sip. The green tea has enough honey to make it palatable. Personally I would prefer a cup of coffee—with enough cream to kill the taste—but since Tabitha isn't supposed to have caffeine, I don't want to be rude and drink coffee in front of her.

Momma and Tabitha are talking about baby things and my attention wanders. Moose comes over and puts his head in my lap, seemingly just as bored with listening to talk of babies as I am.

I rub his soft fur and think about getting a dog for myself. Of course I know I won't do it. I can't.

As a pilot I'm not home enough to take care of a pet. So I have to enjoy my sister-in-law's dog when I'm here.

The back door opens and I hear muffled voices as a couple of guys come inside and hang their coats on a peg by the door. I recognize Jackson's voice as one of them.

I glance up just in time to see my brother walking into the kitchen. My mother gives him a hug, then Jackson introduces us.

I look past my brother, fully expecting to see his latest girl-friend, but instead my gaze locks onto a handsome man about my brother's age, wearing the same pilot's uniform as Jackson. The same Skye Travels embroidered emblem. The same one on my shirts and jackets and cap.

When his gaze meets mine, he doesn't look away. Instead his lips turn up into a slow smile that scatters my heart rate and lets loose a bevy of butterflies in my stomach.

"This is Daniel," my brother's words register somehow in my brain despite the sudden disappearance of all my sense.

I work with pilots all day long every day. Meeting someone new who happens to be a pilot is not something new or unusual for me. It's just an everyday run of the mill occurrence.

Meeting a pilot who has a visceral effect on me, however, is anything but an everyday run of the mill occurrence.

"I'm going to show Daniel to his room," Jackson says.

"Come back down after you get two get settled," Momma says. "I'll make a pot of coffee."

Coffee. What a wonderful idea.

After Jackson and Daniel leave the kitchen, I realize I'm

still holding my cup of tea out in front of me in both hands. Nothing has moved other than my eyes.

Tabitha glances over at me.

"Are you okay?" she asks.

No. "Yes." I set the mug down. "I think I'll have some coffee, too."

Momma is already measuring coffee into the fancy machine someone had brought home last year. I think it had been my brother Reed or maybe it had been Christopher. Definitely one of my brothers.

After I take a sip of tea and set the mug down, I realize my hands are trembling.

I clear my throat and straighten.

"I thought Jackson was bringing home a girl," Tabitha says.

"I think we all just assumed it," Momma said, sitting back down at the breakfast table. "I guess not."

Tabitha glances over at me. I'm keeping my gaze focused on the tea in my mug.

"He's kinda cute," she says in what is obviously intended as a little whisper.

"I hadn't noticed," I say.

I almost miss the glance exchanged between Momma and Tabitha before they go back to talking about cribs and high chairs.

Anyone with any sense at all would know that I was lying. Anybody who took one look at Daniel could see that he was not only kinda cute, he was drop dead gorgeous.

The kind of handsome man that no doubt had women falling at his feet.

And with that slow grin of his, he obviously knows it.

There is nothing more dangerous to a woman's heart than a handsome pilot in uniform.

Coming from a family of pilots AND working with pilots every day, I've been inoculated.

Handsome pilots don't have an affect on me.

Until they do.

Chapter Four

Daniel

I FOLLOW JACKSON FROM THE KITCHEN, THROUGH an open foyer, and up a flight of stairs.

The old house is bigger than it looked like from the outside and it rambles.

"The guest room is right in here," Jackson says, opening the door to a room down a short hallway after turning left at the top of the stairs.

The guest room isn't exactly what I had expected. It looks like it was designed specifically to be a guest room, not just a room with a bed thrown in it or left in it as the case may be which what my parents had done to my room after I left home. My old bedroom was now my mother's craft room with a bed in it.

Besides the bed, there is a nightstand with a lamp and a phone charger. A little computer desk and chair against one wall. Besides the obvious conveniences, it's the view from the large window that instantly draws my attention.

From the window I have an unparalleled view of a meadow stretching to the feet of the tall rugged mountain peaks. The snow-capped mountains have white clouds clustered around them. They look different, already, than they had as we had landed at the runway.

Snowing. That's what Jackson tells me. It's snowing in what he calls the high country.

"Nice view," I say.

"Be careful," Jackson says. "It's easy to get used to."

I turn around and look at him.

He has a rather odd expression on his face and I wonder if we're actually talking about the view.

But then he claps me on the shoulder.

"Let me know if you need anything," he says. "Come on downstairs for coffee when you're ready."

"Will do."

I turn back to the view and realize that it's Jackson's sister that I'm thinking about. She looks a little like Jackson. Same dark hair, hers tumbling around her shoulders. Same eyes except hers are sparkling green. And those lips. Most definitely kissable lips.

He hadn't even told me her name.

All I knew about her is that she's Jackson's sister.

And, oddly enough, that's more than I need to know.

With just one glance I knew that my life as a confirmed bachelor teetered on the edge of being over.

That thought reminds me to check my messages.

Sophia: Are we still getting together for Christmas?

I stare at the message. Sophia and I had broken up two weeks ago. I was pretty sure we had left that in no uncertain terms.

Maybe this is one of those messages that somehow got caught up in cyberspace and only just now landed in my phone.

With all the flying that I do, my phone sometimes gets its wires crossed.

So I ignore the message.

There's no reason to respond to it and embarrass her. Just because we had broken up, doesn't mean I want to embarrass her by answering a text that she sent weeks ago.

I open up my suitcase and hang my clothes on a cast iron rod attached to the wall. An interesting design. Perfect for a guest room.

After washing my face and running a comb through my hair, I change into jeans and a long-sleeve shirt. Should have brought some heavier clothes. Unfortunately I don't own any.

Sounds like I need to take a walk into town. Surely they have a shop that sells sweatshirts.

I put on my boots, lace them up, and deem myself ready to go downstairs for coffee.

It's time to find out more about Jackson's sister.

My friend has been holding out on me. He told me he came from a big family and had sisters, but he didn't tell me he had a beautiful goddess sister.

Chapter Five

Andrea

I'm just finishing up making my coffee just the way I like it with lots of fluffy creamer and a hint of peppermint syrup when I hear the guys coming back downstairs.

I turn around, coffee mug in hand, and my gaze immediately locks onto Daniel's.

"The coffee is ready," Momma tells them. "Help yourself."

What happened to my mother the good hostess? Tabitha has gone back to wrapping gifts and Momma is helping her.

Jackson comes over and grabs two coffee cups from the cabinet.

Daniel stands a few steps behind Jackson, waiting for his cue.

I go with my instinct and hold out my coffee mug to him.

"Thank you," he says, taking the mug from me.

Jackson glances over at me.

"Make me one," I tell him.

Jackson shrugs and puts creamer in the machine.

Empty handed, I go back to my seat at the breakfast table. Daniel follows and sits in the chair next to me.

That's interesting.

I expected him to sit... anywhere else. The table has eight chairs. Tabitha and Momma are sitting side by side. That leaves five chairs on two different sides of the table where he could sit.

But he sits right next to me.

Momma slides a wrapped present and a roll of ribbon in my direction.

"You might as well be useful," she says.

"Gee. Thanks." But I unroll the red ribbon and wrap it around the gift. It shifts when I go to tie it. I don't have the skills my mother and sister-in-law have when it comes to tying bows and such.

What can I say? Growing up, I spent more time with Jackson than my sisters.

Daniel puts his finger on the ribbon to hold it while I tie it.

I look up at him and our eyes lock. His blue eyes have tiny little streaks of indigo that are only visible up close, adding interest to their sparkling intensity.

I forget that I was tying a ribbon and just stare into his

eyes. I'm frozen in place, pinned by his gaze as I hold the ribbon in both hands.

Jackson sets a mug of coffee in front of me.

"Thank you," I say, keeping my gaze on Daniel's.

Daniel smiles at me, a slow smile, that sends my heart rhythm into an erratic state.

"I'm Daniel," he says.

"I know."

"You're Jackson's sister."

"Yes."

He lifts one eyebrow at me questioningly.

"Is that what I should call you?" he asks. "Jackson's sister?"

"Oh." I blink and pulling my gaze from his with a quick glance around the table tells me that three sets of eyes are watching us with curiosity.

"I'm Andrea," I say and tie the ribbon tightly, perhaps too tightly, against his finger.

"It's nice to meet you Andrea," he says, pulling his finger from the tight knot.

I pick up a pair of scissors and snip the ribbon from the roll.

Such a quick exchange and yet I feel heat rising up my cheeks.

I pick up my coffee mug and take a sip of coffee to try and steady myself. I just hope he doesn't notice that my hands are trembling.

The only thing worse than being unsettled by a handsome pilot is letting him know it.

"Do you know how to tie a bow?" I ask him.

He looks at me with confusion.

"Not really," he says.

"Me either."

"But how hard can it be?"

That's all I need to know. With one eyebrow lifted, I slide the gift with the ribbon he and I had just tied into a knot in his direction.

Despite saying he doesn't know how to tie a bow, he deftly does so, making it look better than anything I could do.

"Not bad," I say, sliding the gift back to my mother, shooting her a rather challenging look.

She, however, is no longer paying me any attention.

"How long have you and Jackson known each other?" she asks Daniel.

"Three years," he says. "We started with Skye Travels at the same time."

Jackson is giving his friend an odd look that means nothing to me, but I can tell there's something they aren't saying.

"I see," Momma says. "Well. We're glad to have you join us for Christmas."

"Thank you, Mrs. Flynn."

I hide behind my mug again.

What is it about this guy that has my pulse racing?

As though to thwart my self-reflection, Momma slides another wrapped gift in my direction.

And just like that, we have something of an assembly line going.

I wrap the ribbon around the gifts, Daniel holds his finger on it while I tie it into a knot, and Daniel ties it into a bow.

Who is this friend of my brother who cannot only tie a bow on a Christmas present, but also has my pulse pounding dangerously?

Chapter Six

Daniel

I've only been here with the Flynns for little more than an hour and already I'm in awe of the large family vibe.

They obviously like each other, but they don't take anything off each other.

The three younger ones seem unaffected by their mother or mother-in-law as the case may be, sitting with them. She just sort of blends in with their banter.

My mother always kept herself distant from me and my friends. I have no memories of her ever sitting down and playing a game or engaging in any other leisure activity with

us. She and my father always made sure they were firmly established as the *parents*.

But here I am sitting with just a fraction of Jackson's
family. Tying bows out of ribbons. Who would have
thought it?

I can't even say where I learned to tie a bow. I picked it up
somewhere. My grandmother if memory serves.

I certainly can't say that I ever thought it would come in
handy.

But sitting next to Andrea, who smells like wildflowers, I
have never been so grateful for such a thing that I didn't know
I remembered how to do.

She keeps her gaze off mine for the most part, but she and
I have a system. She wraps the ribbon around the wrapped
present and I put my finger on it to hold it while she ties it into
a knot.

Then I tie the ribbon into a bow.

Jackson leans back in his chair, a coffee mug in his hand
and smirks at me.

I pointedly ignore him.

He invited me here.

And.

He failed to tell me that he had a hot sister.

He can smirk at me all he wants, but he has no one to
blame except himself.

"Where did you learn to tie bows like that?" Tabitha asks.

"My grandmother," I say, going with the most likely
answer. "I spent a lot of time with her when I was growing
up."

"His parents are in Switzerland," Jackson says.

"For Christmas? By themselves?" Mrs. Flynn asks with a tone laced with horror. I get the impression that she can't imagine spending Christmas away from her family.

"They're calling it a second honeymoon," I say. I refrain from telling them that I think that was just an excuse to keep from asking me to join them.

"I see," Mrs. Flynn says. "Do you have brothers and sisters?"

"Just me. I'm an only child."

"That's got to be hard," Tabitha says, placing a hand on her stomach. Probably thinking about making sure she has more than one child.

"Just think how peaceful it must be," Jackson says with a wistfulness in his voice.

Andrea rolls her eyes at him and Tabitha shakes her head. Mrs. Flynn ignores him.

"That's it," she says. "No more presents until someone goes shopping."

She and Tabitha gather up their supplies. Scissors and ribbons and tape, putting everything in a box. Wrapping paper neatly placed in a plastic container.

Tabitha sits back down and checks her phone.

"When is Christopher getting home?" Andrea asks.

"He's scheduled to be here in less than an hour. I think I'll walk down to the airfield and meet him."

"I'll go with you," Mrs. Flynn. "You don't need to go by yourself."

I have to agree with that assessment. A pregnant girl does

not need to be outside walking alone, especially not in the woods by herself.

"It's going to snow," Andrea says.

"We'll be back before it does," Tabitha says.

I'm a little envious of these people who seem to be able to forecast the weather without so much as looking at their weather apps.

"I have some paperwork to do," Jackson says.

"Think I can get some warmer clothes in town?" I ask. "Maybe a sweatshirt?"

"The gift shop has sweatshirts," Tabitha says. "You can also get them at the General Store in town and pretty much anything you might need."

"I'll check it out," I say.

"Someone should go with him," Tabitha says. "He doesn't know his way around." She looks over at me. "Right?"

"Right," I say, caught off-guard. "But Jackson says everything is easy to find."

"It is," Mrs. Flynn chimes in. "But you're a guest and you need a tour guide."

She looks pointedly at Andrea.

Andrea's eyes widen.

"That's a great idea," Tabitha says, looking from me to Andrea and back again as though it hadn't been where she was headed all along.

Chapter Seven

Andrea

MAYBE JACKSON WAS RIGHT. MAYBE BEING AN ONLY child would have been a blessing in disguise.

But... it's a little late. And now that my family is doubling in size as my older brothers and sisters get married, I'm rather stuck with being part of a big family, annoying as they may be at times.

And as annoying as they can be, it's a little hard to complain when they insist I show my brother's handsome friend around. Not that I would ever in a million years admit that to any of them.

"Do you have a coat?" I ask Daniel as we head toward the back door where we keep our coats.

"Sure," he says, taking a light jacket from one of the pegs.

"That's not a coat," I say. "That's a jacket."

"Hence the trip into town," he says.

"You don't have to buy a coat," she says and grabs one of the heavy coats from one of the pegs. Hands it to me.

"Whose coat is this?" I ask.

"I don't know. One of the guys."

"Shouldn't we ask them?"

"One of the perks of having a big family is not having to ask."

"Huh," I say and shrug into the coat. It feels new. I'm not even sure it's ever been worn much.

"You don't have to come with me," he says. "I'm sure I can find my way around."

"Trying to get me in trouble?" I ask.

"You do have a good point," he says as we step out into the cold. "Do you ever get used to this?"

"The cold? I find it invigorating." I glance over at him. "You're from Houston, right?"

"Born and raised."

"Do you get used to the heat?"

"No," he says. "I could do without it. The winters are good though."

"I'll take the cold weather any day." I pull a wool cap out of my pocket and put it over my head.

He grins at me.

"What?"

"Nothing. It's just you couldn't pay a Houston girl to mess up her hair like that."

"Now you're telling me that my hair is messy."

He puts his hands in his coat pockets and grins at me.

"Just the opposite actually," he said. "I think it's adorable."

"Now you're just making fun of me."

"I know Jackson is your brother, but I'm not. So I would never make fun of you."

I look over at him sideways wondering what my brother has to do with anything.

"I don't think he ever mentioned you," I say.

"He never mentioned you either."

"Really? That's hard to believe as much as Jackson talks."

"Oh. He talks. I knew he was from a big family. Everyone knows that. He just didn't tell anyone that he specifically has you for a sister."

"I don't know why he would." I tuck a strand of hair behind an ear and straighten my wool cap. A wool cap I'm now questioning. It's not exactly the most attractive thing to wear on my head, but I honestly never gave it much thought. It was always just something I wore when I was here in Alpine Falls. Never in Denver and certainly never when I'm working.

The lodge comes into view with smoke wafting from its two fireplaces.

"You picked a good time to visit," I say, purposely changing the subject.

"Why is that?"

"We do Christmas right."

"I understand it's a destination place for people at Christmastime."

"A lot of people do come here every year."

"My parents could have come here."

"And yet they went to Switzerland."

We reach the back door to the inn and Daniel pulls it open.

"You didn't want to go with them?" I ask.

"I wasn't invited."

The warm air inside the lodge is inviting.

"Right. The whole honeymoon thing."

"Something like that."

I look over at him, but let that go as I begin my tour.

"Here on the right where there's music is the restaurant. We call it a lounge by night and a café by day."

"Sounds a little confusing," he says.

"You get used to it."

We keep walking. Someone picked old jazz music for the jukebox which always seems to fit the old lodge better than any modern music.

"And now we step into the quiet part of the lodge. As you can see, the big fireplace is one of the focal points."

The stone fireplace, open on all four sides with cast iron screens has comfortable armchairs surrounding it, good for just relaxing or reading. At the moment there is no one sitting there.

"That Christmas tree looks like it's the focal point at the moment."

And he is right. There is a couple posing for a photo in front of the tree. It has the usual oversized gifts beneath it. Empty boxes that my sisters wrap up every year and place beneath the tree.

"Anything in those boxes?" he asks.

"What do you think?"

"I honestly don't know."

I glance over at him. Is he really serious about that?

"They're just for decoration."

"Is the fire always going?" he asks.

"Good question. Yes. Except in the middle of the night."

"Must take a lot of firewood."

"You have no idea. But people really like it. We actually have high school boys whose whole job is to keep the fireplaces clean and burning."

"Must be hard to do at the same time."

"It is," I say ignoring his attempt at humor. "We all took our turn at it growing up."

"Yeah. Jackson told me you all worked at the lodge growing up."

"So he does talk about his family."

"At times."

"That's our sister Arabella behind the front desk," I tell him. "She's the manager but she always ends up behind the desk."

"She must be good at what she does."

"Scary good."

I slow down as we near the front doors.

"And on the left is the gift shop if you'd like to look around."

"I'll come back," he says. "I don't want to interrupt my very interesting tour."

"It's a good idea for us to go and get back before it snows anyway."

One of the valets opens the front doors and we step outside back into the startling cold.

Daniel pulls the collar up on his coat.

"Still not used to it," he says.

I laugh, no longer able to ignore his humor.

Funny. He's a funny guy.

A handsome pilot who makes me laugh.

Probably not a good combination at this particular point in time. If ever.

Chapter Eight

Daniel

As we walk along the path that takes us from the lodge to downtown Alpine Falls, I'm glad I have Andrea with me as my tour guide.

Not that I couldn't have found my way alone. I can always find a way to get where I need to go. I am most definitely not afraid to ask for directions.

But my little tour is infinitely more interesting walking with a pretty girl than it would be walking alone.

I spend enough time doing things by myself to appreciate someone taking the time to show me around.

And if that someone happens to be the sister of my good friend, then that's all the better.

I still maintain that Jackson should have warned me he had a pretty sister.

They have the same eyes, only different colors. That's taking me a little while to get used to.

Not that I mind. Although it occurs to me to wonder if kissing Andrea would be weird.

Same eyes and all.

I decide that particular thought is over my head at the moment. Not something I should even be contemplating even in a philosophical manner of thinking.

It doesn't take long to walk to downtown Alpine Falls.

"I didn't realize there was an Amtrak station here," I say, looking over at the train station and the silver train sitting at the depot. People getting off. Looking a little lost as they locate their luggage.

"A person can get here any way they like. Plane. Train. Automobile."

"You're lucky to be part of something like this."

"Like this town?" she looks at me a bit askance.

"Your family. Your heritage. I don't have that.

"Right. You're an only child."

"Yes," I say. "But it's not just that. I had cousins and grandparents." Even if I didn't see them all that often. "It's this sense of place that I don't have."

She nods. "It is comforting to know that it'll always be here. Hopefully with our family being as big as it is, there will always be someone who will want to continue with the lodge. That we'll always have someplace to come home to."

"Surely it's not in any kind of danger."

"No," she says. "It's a thriving business. It's just things change with time. I hope it's always here for us."

"I'm sure it will be. Something this old and established is likely to remain."

"I like your optimism. Now," she says. "On your right you can see the General Store."

I follow her gaze. The General Store is much smaller than I had hoped. It's possible I'll have to go online and place an order for the basic things I'm going to need while I'm here.

If I'd been smart, I would have thought to shop for wool socks and warm clothes ahead of time, but even if I'd thought about it, it would have been challenging to find them in Houston where the weather rarely gets cold.

"Around the corner is an ice cream shop. And a Hungry Biscuit just opened up."

"What's a Hungry Biscuit?" I ask, trying to keep a straight face.

"It's a local chain restaurant. It's actually quite good. You should try it while you're here."

"I'll do that." I glance at my watch. "Is it too early to have lunch?"

"Now?"

"Sure. Why not? You said it's good and it's the least I can do to show my appreciation for the tour."

"You don't have to worry about that," she says.

There's something that strikes me as a little odd about that statement.

"What do you mean?"

"My family gives tours to anyone who requests one."

"And here I was thinking I was special."

She looks sideways at me.

"If it makes you feel any better" she says. "I rarely give tours."

"That does make me feel better."

"Do you want to go shopping or have lunch first?"

"Lunch," I say. "Always go for food first. Just in case something happens."

"You sound like my brothers."

"Well. We are all pilots."

She studies me from beneath her eyelashes.

"I don't think it's that. I can't put my finger on it."

"I'm sure it'll come to you," I say.

"I'm sure."

We reach the Hungry Biscuit and I open the door for her to walk through.

We are immediately assaulted by Christmas music spilling out of hidden speakers.

"Guess we're early," she says. "It's usually crowded."

"That's a good thing, right?"

"I don't mind the crowds. Reminds me of being in the city."

The hostess leads us to a table in the back.

"Denver?" I ask, considering.

"Mostly."

"Skye Travels has an office in Denver."

"I know," she says, picking up her menu and hiding behind it.

"What do you usually get here?" I ask.

"Most people get the hamburger and fries."

"Are they good?"

"I think so."

The server stops at our table.

Andrea orders a hamburger and fries, extra pickles.

"I'll have the same," I say.

She lifts an eyebrow at me.

"Keeps things simple," I say.

"You're not like most pilots," she says.

"No? How is that?"

"Most pilots like to pretend that they're in charge."

"Because they usually are."

"Hmph. Good point."

"But we don't have to always be in charge. Sometimes it's nice to just sit back and let someone else make the hard decisions."

"Like what to order for lunch?" she asks, looking at me sideways.

"Sometimes the smallest decisions can be the hardest."

"You're probably right," she says.

I just grin.

"So tell me," she says. "What do you think so far? About Alpine Falls?"

"I think it's absolutely charming."

"Do you think you could live here?" she asks.

The question leaves me feeling a little stunned and it must show on my face.

"It's just a question. A lot of people from the city think

they could live here, but they quickly get bored. I'm just checking your boredom quotient."

I laugh.

"I don't know. I would say no, but if I'm honest with myself, I have to admit that I rarely get out and do anything even though I live in Houston. When I'm in city, I tend to spend it doing things like laundry."

"You don't make being a pilot sound nearly as exciting as people think it is," she says.

"I hate to disillusion you."

"You don't have to worry about that."

The server drops off a basket of chips and two little bowls of salsa, one for each of us.

"You've already become disillusioned?" I ask.

"Something like that."

She's looking at me with big green eyes that could send a man looking for rocks to climb over to get to her.

If I remember correctly from my college days, there used to be some kind of code against a guy hooking up with his best friend's sister.

I don't know whether that's still a thing or not.

But. In my defense, Jackson is not my *best* friend. Just a good friend. And in the great scheme of friendships, he's a new friend.

Maybe that makes him an exception.

I should not be thinking about dating Andrea.

She lives in Alpine Falls and I live in Houston.

I am not the kind of guy who likes long distance relationships.

I don't maintain girlfriends in cities outside of Houston, despite the common preconception of pilots everywhere.

I figure there are enough girls for me to date in Houston without going outside my geographic region.

Being a pilot, as far as I'm concerned does not give me the right to pursue women that I have no chance or inclination of forming a lasting relationship with.

I don't tell anyone this, of course. I would be banned from the brotherhood of pilots.

Nonetheless, Andrea has me wondering.

She has me wondering about a lot of things.

Things I probably shouldn't even be thinking about, much less wondering about.

Like, for one, what would it be like to kiss her?

"So," I say, to distract myself. "Besides coming to the Hungry Biscuit, what do people do for fun around here?"

Chapter Nine

Andrea

I HADN'T ASKED TO BE SADDLED WITH SHOWING Daniel around town, but now that I was I don't mind.

In fact, I find him to be delightful.

It didn't even bother me that he was a pilot. Not really, anyway.

I am, of course, acutely aware of it.

Being a pilot myself and having spent my life around pilots, starting with my brothers and then college and then work, I have a pretty good handle on the way they think.

It's not that I think that way, being a pilot, but I *understand* it.

I understand the lifestyle. The viewpoint. And all that.

But still. Daniel seems... different.

I like him.

My brother should have told me about him. Not that it would have made any difference.

There is no way I could have anticipated actually liking one of my brother's friends.

Sure. My sister, Bianca is married to one of Jackson's friends from Alpine Falls, but that was different. They'd all grown up together.

Daniel was from Houston.

Daniel had no way of understanding what it was like living in Alpine Falls. That was evident in his question.

"What do people do?" I answer his question with a question.

"Yeah. You know. Just in general."

"I think most people come here to get away from doing things."

He looks at me with something akin to disbelief, so I give him some things people might do while they're here.

"Some people go hiking or picnicking. At Christmas, they come for the activities."

"What kind of activities?"

"We have a tree decorating contest."

He lifts an eyebrow.

"I know. it doesn't sound exciting, but people enjoy it. We also have a masquerade ball on Christmas Eve."

"Christmas Eve? Aren't most people with their families?"

"Not here. Unless they bring them or they live here."

"Huh."

"Mostly people come here to relax. To enjoy nature. Or to just sit in front of the fireplace and read a good book."

"Okay," he says. "That doesn't sound too bad."

"It's not." I smile.

"What's it like living here?" he asks.

I pick up a chip. Break it in half and dip it into the salsa.

"It's like any other small town. Everybody knows everybody's business."

He sits back and looks around.

"So you know all these people here right now?"

I glance around.

"I don't know a single person in here."

"So... they're all tourists?"

"I don't know. Maybe. Some of them."

"But you just said everyone knows everyone."

"Okay." So he's going to be smart. "We know people in our age group until we move away for college or whatever. Then we don't." I shrug. I think I made that fairly simple and clear.

"I would think you would at least see someone you know," he persists.

"Like I said, that changes after you leave here."

"You sound like you're speaking from experience."

"I am. I don't live in Alpine Falls."

Chapter Ten

Daniel

"Wait," I say.

Andrea takes a sip of her drink, then looks at me with a rather self-assured expression.

As a matter of fact, I can see a whole lot of Jackson in her right now. I've seen him wear that same expression.

"I thought you lived here."

"I grew up here."

"Where do you live?"

"Denver."

"I see. Well. That's unexpected."

"Andrea Flynn?"

Andrea turns and looks at a man who just walked up to our table.

"Donald? What are you doing here?"

"I live here."

"Right." Andrea glances at me. "This is Donald. We went to school together. Donald, this is my friend Daniel."

"Good to meet you," I say.

She introduced me as her friend, not her brother's friend and even not a guest of the lodge, which technically I'm not.

It's such a little thing. She probably didn't even think anything of it, but it seems like a big deal to me.

"I thought you were an accountant," Andrea says to Donald.

"I am. I drive into Glenwood Springs to work."

"Oh. I'm sorry."

Donald smiles. "I don't mind. The wife and kids love it here, so it's worth it. It's good to see you again."

"You too." After he returns to his family, I turn back to Daniel. "Well. He recognized me."

"How could he not?" I ask. "You went to school together."

"I haven't seen him in almost ten years."

"Trust me," I say. "A guy doesn't forget the prettiest girl in class."

I make a face. "Now I truly know that you're a pilot through and through."

"Why would you say that?"

"Because you haven't met anyone else in my class."

"I don't have to," I say. And yes, she's right. It is the kind of thing a pilot would say when he's hitting on a girl. But I don't have to see anyone else in her class to know that she's the prettiest.

Even if a hundred other women walked through that door right now, I can guarantee that there wouldn't be another girl I would find more attractive than Andrea.

The server brings our food out and our conversation skips right along to something else.

I'd come here to spend Christmas with Jackson and his family.

I had not come here to fall for his sister.

Sometimes the most life-changing things happen when a person isn't expecting them.

And meeting Jackson's sister was one of those life-changing things.

I'd only known her for a few hours, but sometimes that's all it takes.

Chapter Eleven

Andrea

"You have to get one of these," I say, picking up a wool cap with a pompom on top of it.

"Oh no. You are not getting me into one of those hats."

I run a hand along a similar, very similar hat, on top of my head. "And what's wrong with my hat?"

"Nothing. If you're a girl."

"Okay. I set the wool cap back down. "Don't complain to me when your ears freeze off."

He picks up the cap. "Well, it does have the Alpine Lodge logo on it."

"Never mind," I say. "You've insulted my hat."

"I'm getting it," he says, adding it to the stack he's carrying in his arms.

He bought some waterproof boots at the General Store and a scarf and a set of gloves, but nothing else there suited him.

So I'd brought him to the Alpine Lodge gift shop. We had the best quality things anyway. I might be a little biased, but it was true.

As the manager, my sister-in-law, Tabitha, made sure of it.

"Do you see anything else I'm going to need?" he asks.

"Not right now. I think you have the basics. You can always come back."

"I can, at that."

He takes his things to the checkout counter.

"Did you find everything you needed?" Mrs. Smith asks. Mrs. Smith had come out of retirement to help out during the holidays while Tabitha's pregnant.

"More than I need," Daniel says, glancing at me.

I just smile.

"You have to watch that one," Mrs. Smith says. "She has good strong Flynn blood."

I don't even know what she means by that, but it sounds good to me.

While she rings up Daniel's purchase, I wander over to check out the snow globes. One by one, I pick them up and turn them over before setting them back down.

I always like to think that they need to be turned on a regular basis.

As a child, I'd believed that if I could get all of them turned over and snowing at the same time, that it would actually snow outside.

I'd never been fast enough to test out that little theory of mine. It was just as well, since I'm sure I would have been sorely disappointed.

"These are nice," Daniel says coming over to see what I'm doing.

I tell him my childhood theory.

"Let's test it out," he says, setting his shopping bags on the floor at his feet.

"I don't think it counts if—"

Never mind. He's already doing it. I start at the other end and meet him in the middle.

"We got them all going," he says.

"They're beautiful."

"It must be snowing outside, right?"

"You're going to kill my childhood magical belief system," I say, but I follow him into the lobby and over to the window.

I gasp.

It's snowing. Not much. Just the first fluffy flakes that suggest snow is coming.

"See," he says. "Not ruined. In fact..." He turns to me with a grin. "You were right."

Gazing into Daniel's smiling eyes, I can't look away. I don't want to look away.

I'd never, not once, told anyone about my childhood belief about the snow globes. They would have made fun of me, I'm certain of it.

I'm also certain that I shouldn't have told Daniel. If I'd

thought about it a second longer, I wouldn't have. He caught me in a weak moment.

I'd only known him for the span of a few hours at most, but there was something about him that made me trust him.

Made me want to tell him my innermost secrets.

And that was something that just didn't happen with me.

Chapter Twelve

Daniel

I'D HOPED TO SEE SNOW WHILE I WAS IN ALPINE Falls, but it was still surprising and quite delightful.

I'd seen snow, sure, just not in Houston and since most of my flights were in the south, it wasn't something I saw on a regular basis.

I was looking forward to my week here, more and more by the minute.

It wasn't just the snow. It was the delightfulness of Jackson's sister.

I didn't want to tell her that I was as surprised as she was that it was snowing when we left the gift shop. I didn't actually believe that it came from the magic of the snow globes.

I considered myself to be a level-headed, practical guy. Magic wasn't in my vocabulary.

But seeing the delight on her face had me believing in a different kind of magic.

The magic of love at first sight.

I had never experienced love at first sight and I had not been sure I believed in it.

Until now.

"Come on," I say, taking her hand and leading her toward the front doors.

The valet smiles and holds the door open for us.

"It's snowing out there," he says with a smile.

"I know." We walk out into the falling snow.

White fluffy flakes drift gently in the wind like leaves falling from trees on an autumn day.

"It's just a little flurry," Andrea says, but a little smile plays about her lips.

"And what's not to like?" I ask, looking into her green eyes.

She blinks as a snowflake lands on her eyelashes.

"Nothing," she says.

I could kiss her right now. Right here.

The valet opens the door, stealing that opportunity away.

"Miss Andrea," he says. "Miss Arabella is looking for you."

She shrugs. "Duty calls."

We go back inside and find Arabella behind the front desk where Andrea predicted she would be.

"Hey," Arabella says with a curious glance in my direction. "You must be Daniel."

"That's right." I shouldn't be surprised. Of course she would know I was here. I was staying in her home. "Nice to meet you."

"What do you need us to do?" Andrea asks.

I like the sound of her saying *we*.

Hanging out with her is much more interesting than hanging out with my friend Jackson.

"I need you to go up to the attic and see if you can find any records."

"Records? We keep records in the attic?"

"No. Not that kind of records. You know. Vinyl. Music."

"Oh. Right. I know what records are," Andrea says. "I just don't know what you need them for."

"Well. Somebody gave our brother, Jackson, a record player and he donated it to the lodge."

"Why?" Andrea asks.

"No imagination," Arabella says to me.

"Oh. I have to respectfully disagree with that," I say, looking over at Andrea. "I say she definitely has a good imagination."

One that I want to explore to the fullest.

Chapter Thirteen

Andrea

VINYL RECORDS.

From the attic.

"Where are you going to play records?" I ask, stalling on purpose.

A couple of teenage girl sitting in front of the large four-sided fireplace laugh and I realize they're looking this way. Specifically at Daniel.

He doesn't seem to notice.

"Jackson is setting it up in the lounge for now. We're working out other plans," Arabella says. "Look for Christmas records, specifically."

"What makes you think there are records in the attic?" I ask.

"They haven't been used for decades," Arabella says, sliding the attic key across the counter. "It's the most logical place."

"It's okay," Daniel says. "I'll go up. Help you find them and bring them down."

I look into Daniel's smiling blue eyes. He has no idea what he's getting into.

"Get Jackson to go," I tell my sister, pulling my gaze away from Daniel back to her.

She narrows her eyes at me and I know the answer.

Jackson won't go.

My brother refuses to go into the attic.

"Okay. Fine. Let's just get it over with." I grab the key and turn on my heel.

Daniel looks confused, but he follows me.

He doesn't understand.

We cross the lobby, passing the girls, still watching him, in front of the fireplace. I feel an irrational little spurt of jealousy. They're just teenage girls, though and I brush it aside.

Besides, I have no right to be jealous. Not of anyone. No claim whatsoever on my brother's friend.

We walk past the tall blue spruce Christmas tree standing in the lobby. It stands tall, towering all the way to the upstairs balcony. It's decorated in clear twinkling lights like it always is.

Over the years guests have started bringing Christmas decorations from their part of the country and leaving them on the tree. Adding a little piece of home to the tree where they're spending Christmas.

I see a few new ones since last year. There is a golden beehive from Utah. A boot-shaped one wearing a red Santa hat from Louisiana. Another boot-shaped one, this one from Texas.

And as usual, there are a dozen wrapped gifts underneath the tree, some of them super large boxes that I know have nothing in them.

"So what do you have against the attic?" Daniel asks as we start up the wide staircase leading to the second floor.

"Nothing," I say, not looking at him.

"Doesn't seem like nothing."

We turn right, going down the hallway toward the attic door.

"It's just something I don't..." I stop in mid-sentence as the burning candles in the glass sconces flicker. The candles are behind glass. They should not flicker.

Daniel doesn't seem to notice.

Most people don't, but then as far as I know, the candle flames don't flicker when most people walk past.

If they do, they either don't notice or don't think it's worth saying anything about.

But I notice. And I swallow a nervous lump in my throat.

I keep walking, knowing that my purposeful stride toward the attic slows as we near the door.

My hands tremble a little as I go to put the key in the lock.

Daniel places a hand over mine.

"Wait," he says. "What's happening? Why are you so nervous about going into the attic?"

I shake my head and close my eyes.

My family doesn't normally talk about it to guests. We have our reasons. But I see no reason not to tell Daniel.

I open my eyes and turn around.

"See those candles?" The candles aren't flickering now.

He follows my gaze.

"Yes. They're nice."

I don't disagree. They are nice. But...

"Did you notice them flickering when we walked by?"

"I guess. I didn't notice anything out of the ordinary."

"They aren't supposed to flicker." I lower my voice to a whisper and look into his eyes.

"Why not?"

I shake my head. "They're behind glass."

"Maybe there's a breeze—"

"No. There's no logical explanation." I run a hand through my hair and blow out a breath. "We've looked."

He looks at me quizzically.

Leaning forward, keeping my voice low, I tell him.

"The attic is haunted."

Chapter Fourteen

Daniel

ANDREA AND I ARE STANDING OUTSIDE A LOCKED attic door at the end of the hallway on the second floor of the lodge.

There are soft overhead lights, but thick, chunky candles add an old-fashioned ambiance that fits with the historical nature of the lodge.

"Haunted?" I repeat what Andrea just told me.

"Sh." She puts a finger against her lips.

"What?" I bite back a laugh, but I lower my voice anyway. "Ghosts can hear us even if we whisper."

Her finger against her lips draws attention to them, making me want to kiss them.

"Probably." She puts her hands on her hips. "But still... We don't talk about it."

"Why not?"

"My parents... I think... maybe my grandparents... decided they didn't want the Alpine Lodge to be known as a haunted house."

"So. Wait. Your family can see the ghosts? But guests can't?"

"Yes. The guests don't say anything about it. So..." She runs a hand nervously through her hair. "Actually there's just one ghost." She lowers her voice. "Her name is Abigail."

I look back down the hallway at the candles. Still not flickering.

"That must be very lonely for her."

Andrea frowns. "For Abigail?"

"Yeah. Being a ghost without any friends must be really lonely."

"I never thought of it that way."

"Sure. That's why she wants to... interact with you all."

"Maybe." Andrea looks at the key in her hand.

"But... this isn't the attic."

"I know. It's hard to understand, much less explain."

"So if she messes with the candles, what's with the attic?"

"It's the attic," she says with a shrug. "It's where most people see her."

"Have you seen her?"

"No," Andrea says quickly with a little shiver. "I would be terrified."

"Why? Has she ever hurt anyone?"

"No. Of course not. It's just... She's a ghost." She whispers that last sentence and I have to bite back a laugh.

"Well," I say. "You're in luck. I'm not afraid of ghosts."

"Have you ever seen one?" she asks, narrowing her eyes at me.

"No. But I think it would be interesting."

"You sound like Arabella and James."

"Really? How so?" I lean against the wall, keeping one eye on the candles, hoping to see them flicker.

"They swear she was their matchmaker."

"Wow. This just gets more and more interesting."

Andrea smiles. The first time I've seen her smile since Arabella asked her to come up to the attic.

"Do you think maybe your sister is trying to return the favor?"

A door opens and closes halfway down the hallway and couple walk hand in hand toward the stairs.

"What do you mean?" Andrea asks.

"Maybe she's hoping Abigail will play matchmaker with... you." I almost said *us*. It had been on the tip of my tongue to say it, but I caught myself at the last moment.

"Arabella just wants the records. She's all about business."

As though to punctuate her thoughts, she turns the door-knob and with a deep breath, pushes open the door.

It creaks like a door in a haunted house. A shiver runs down my spine, in spite of what I'd said earlier about not being afraid.

"Come on," I say, taking Andrea's hand.

Going into a haunted attic is about as good an excuse an any to hold her hand.

I'll take the opportunity wherever I can find it.

Chapter Fifteen

Andrea

I'D HARDLY BEEN IN THE ATTIC SINCE THAT DAY Jackson and I sneaked in here to play. He had been twelve and I had been ten.

I'd been up a couple of times with Arabella, but Jackson refused to come back after that day.

I remembered so many details. I had run downstairs to use the restroom. Jackson had stayed. He was looking for something. I can't even remember what it was now. When I came back up the narrow stairs into the attic, Jackson had been standing there, white as a sheet.

"What's wrong?" I asked.

"Did you see someone leave?" he asked.

"No. When?"

"Just now. On the stairs. Did you pass someone on the stairs?"

"No. What's wrong with you?"

"There was a girl here. Wearing a white dress. She talked to me."

I looked over my shoulder. I hadn't seen anyone.

"What did she say?"

"She said her name was Abigail."

"That's all?"

Jackson shook his head, but he didn't tell me what she said. He'd never told me, not to this day, what Abigail had told him."

"Jackson saw her," I tell Daniel as we're halfway up the stairs.

"No way." He stopped and looked at me. I could tell he didn't know whether or not to believe me. Or what to think.

"He did."

"When?"

"He was twelve, I think."

"So he won't come up here."

"You're very perceptive," I say, glancing over at him.

He just shrugs and starts walking again.

At the top of the stairs, the attic opens up in front of us. It's one big wide open space, about as large as the lobby below.

There are two dormer windows on the front of the house. Not very big, but enough to let in some natural light and I can see that the snow is falling a little heavier now.

Even though the attic is one big room, it's divided into

sections. There's a section with furniture. A section with old trunks full of discarded clothes and other personal items. And a section of Christmas decorations.

The Christmas decorations section is mostly empty boxes at the moment since most of the decorations are scattered about the inn.

"Where do you suggest we start looking?" Daniel asks.

They won't be with the furniture or the Christmas decorations.

"Maybe over there with the trunks," I say.

"There are a lot of boxes here," he says.

"They should be marked. Most things are labeled."

We start looking at the stacks of boxes. Daniel moves a couple of them off the top so we can see the labels written on the sides.

"I guess if it's *not* marked," he says. "We need to open it up and look inside."

I shrug. "We should have brought a marker so we can write on them after we open them."

"I can run down and get one," Daniel says with a straight face, pulling a box down.

"Very funny. Don't even think about leaving me up here by myself."

He stops and smiles at me. Then he looks serious.

"I wouldn't even consider it."

The way he's looking at me. Kind and understanding. And something else. I see something in his eyes. Something that makes me want to be the only girl he has ever and will ever look at like this.

Chapter Sixteen

Daniel

I've learned so much about my friend, Jackson, today.

I learned that he's terrified of ghosts. So much so that he won't go into the attic at the inn.

I learned that he's generous with his family. Somebody gave him a record player and he donated it to the lodge.

And finally, I learned that he has a sister who is a beautiful goddess. Something he shamefully kept from one of his best friends.

I suppose I don't really blame him for keeping Andrea a secret from his pilot friends. If I had a sister like Andrea, I'd do what I could to protect her, too. Especially from the likes of pilots.

But I don't have a sister, so it's a little hard for me to do more than speculate what it must be like to have a sister that must have boys lined up to take her out.

"I think I found them," I say, sliding over a box that had been buried at the bottom of a stack.

It's even labeled *records.*

"It's either vinyl records or paperwork," Andrea says, kneeling next to me. "Is it heavy?"

"Yes, but I guess it could be either one."

"Let's take a look," she says, lifting the lid.

"Look at that."

A whole stack of vinyl records with bright sleeves on them. I had forgotten just how important the packaging was back when people bought records.

"We found them," she says, sitting back on her heels.

"Arabella said Christmas, right?"

"Right."

"Do you want me to...?" I won't lie. I'm itching to put my hands on them. This is like a treasure trove.

"Sure," she says. "Please. Go ahead."

"My grandfather had a record player and he taught me how to use it. We had some nice evenings sitting, listening to records, talking."

"That sounds nice," she says, wistfully.

I start going through the records, picking them up one at the time, handling them with reverence.

"It was nice. I miss him."

"I'm sorry," Andrea says.

"It's okay. I have wonderful memories."

And years of therapy to get me to the point of appreciating them without the heartbreaking sadness that had come automatically.

"There's a Christmas one," Andrea says, picking up the next one.

It's a really old cover. Maybe as old as the 1920s.

"It's a—" I stop, forgetting what I was going to say.

Soft music plays in the background.

"Can I see the back?" I ask.

"Sure." She hands over the record.

And there it is on the list. The song I'm hearing.

"Do you hear that?" I ask, looking up at her.

"Do I hear what?" Andrea asks, her face draining of color.

I lean forward, pointing to the song on the list.

"That song is playing."

"Where?"

"In the attic. Right here. Right now."

Andrea shakes her head. "I don't hear it."

I grin. "I think I'm getting a private concert."

"Let's go," Andrea says, her eyes wide.

I look down at the records in the box. There are so many yet to see.

"But there are other…"

"No."

"Records."

"I'm serious," she says. "If you're hearing music, we need to leave."

"Okay. What about the box?"

"Leave it. Arabella can come up here and..." She waves a hand. "Do whatever she wants to do with it."

Bringing the Christmas record with me, I follow Andrea across the attic to the stairs.

The song ends abruptly and it crosses my mind that I might have imagined it.

Maybe I'd wanted to see or hear a sign of the ghost so badly that my brain had manifested it.

I don't believe in that kind of hoodoo though. I'm a pilot with both feet firmly planted on the ground.

Ironic, I know.

But even though I believe in what I can see and touch, I have an open mind about all things.

After all, if two people can love each other as much as my grandparents had loved each other, then there is most certainly more to this world than what we can see and touch.

Andrea, however, doesn't seem to hold the same sentiment.

She practically races down the stairs. When we reach the second floor and close the door, her breathing is coming in shallow gasps.

"Hey," I say. "Everything is okay."

"I know," she says, barely able to catch her breath.

I put a hand on her chest, just below her neck.

"Breathe with me," I say, looking into her green eyes. Eyes that currently aren't exactly focused.

I take a deep breath. Let it out.

On the second breath, she picks up my rhythm and breaths with me.

"That's good," I say. "It's okay."

She nods. "Yes. Okay."

Her green eyes focus on mine and I feel something stir deep inside me. A visceral reaction. This is no ordinary girl.

This is the girl I want to marry.

I don't care that we just met. I know everything I need to know.

She's the one.

It's crystal clear and quite simple.

Her breathing is back to normal now and our gazes are still locked.

I lean forward, my breath mingling with hers. Her eyes flutter closed, her lips part.

But I don't kiss her. Not yet.

I sweep a strand of hair behind her ear.

I want to take my time.

Once I kiss Andrea, I will have had my very last first kiss.

Chapter Seventeen

Andrea

My world tilts beneath my feet.

I put a hand on Daniel's wrist to steady myself.

My eyes drift closed as he shifts toward me and I lean in for the kiss I sense is coming.

I feel his breath mingling with mine.

But as the clock on the first floor chimes the hour, he moves back. I feel him shifting away, leaving me feeling the loss of his presence.

I blink open my eyes and look at him, feeling confused and a little disappointed. Bereft even.

He smiles and takes my hand, leading me toward the top of the stairs.

I absently notice that the candles aren't flickering. There is no sign of Abigail except for the music Daniel had heard.

Hearing music is a whole new phenomenon. One that I haven't heard anyone say anything about.

I've heard a lot of things, but never anything about someone hearing music. If it really was music, wouldn't I have heard it, too? I'm the one with Flynn blood and the Flynns have always been the ones Abigail has shown herself to.

Except on rare occasions. Like when Arabella's now husband, James, saw Abigail. From the little bit I'd gathered from hearing them talk, he hadn't even known she was a ghost when he had a conversation with her.

It wasn't something we talked about. No one wanted us to be known as a haunted house. That attracted a whole different set of guests than my family was going for.

My family wanted to attract guests who not only drove in or came in on the train, but those who came in on private jets and private helicopters.

Ghost hunters would come with their equipment, disrupting the quiet ambiance of the lodge.

It made perfect sense to me.

As we reach the bottom of the stairs, Daniel releases my hand and we walk straight to the front desk where Arabella is working.

We wait while she finishes checking in a guest, an older man with a cute little terrier sitting at his feet.

"Do you know if Mrs. McAtee has checked in yet?" he asks.

"I don't know," Arabella says. "Are you supposed to be meeting her here?"

"I sure do hope so," the man says with a grin. "We met here at the lodge last year. She says she comes here every Christmas. I'm really hoping to see her again." He looks down at his dog. "She even talked me into getting Astro."

Astro barks once.

"Getting Astro was one of the best things I've done for myself since I lost my wife. That and coming here for Christmas last year."

"I see. He's adorable," Arabella says. "You go on up and get settled in. Then come down and sit at the fireplace. Now I can't tell you if she's a guest here or not, but if I see her, I can point her in your direction."

"That's perfect. Thank you so much, Dear."

Daniel and I walk around the counter.

"Mrs. McAtee has a boyfriend," I say. "I didn't see that coming."

"It's sweet," Arabella says. "She's here, too, but I can't tell him that.

"I know. But I can't wait to see them together. It's so sweet. And he got a puppy."

"We're becoming a romantic destination," Arabella says, looking right at Daniel.

"That's not a bad thing is it?" Daniel asks.

I bite my lip. I know what my sister is thinking. She's thinking it's better than being known as a haunted lodge.

"We'll take it," Arabella says. "I see you found a Christmas record. Is that the only one?"

Daniel and I exchange a glance.

"There might be others," I say. "We had to leave."

Arabella narrows her eyes at me, then glances at Daniel.

"Something happened?"

I glance at my watch. "We're going to take this to the lounge and see how it works."

"You didn't tell her," Daniel says once we're out of earshot.

"It didn't seem like the right time," I say.

It wasn't something I wanted to talk about right now. I had something else I wanted to think about.

And it had something to do with the blue-eyed handsome man walking along beside me.

Just when I'd thought he was going to kiss me, he'd stopped.

Chapter Eighteen

Daniel

PUTTING THE RECORD ON THE PLAYER AND dropping the needle onto the vinyl reminded me of the evenings spent with my grandfather.

Good memories. Sitting in front of the fireplace with him and my grandmother. They would talk about all the things they had done when they were younger. Like how they'd met. The way they had run off in the night to elope.

Since then, I'd always thought of eloping as the most romantic way to get married.

It was private and intimate and a moment just between two people. That's how they had described it anyway. And they had been happy. Married for sixty years.

I missed them every day.

I was quickly getting too old to get to the sixty year anniversary with anyone, but it could happen. Besides, it wasn't the number of years, it was the quality of the years.

"This is good quality music," I say, looking over at where Andrea stands next to me.

The strains of the music fill the lounge. It's mid-afternoon, so there are only a few other guests. We almost have it to ourselves.

Clear lights twinkle on a blue spruce Christmas tree near the table where the record player is set up. Clear twinkling lights and red ornaments. Stacks of gifts wrapped in red beneath the tree. The scent of the real blue spruce tree blends with the scent of the freshly chopped firewood stacked in front of the fireplace.

"I'm a little surprised," she says, closing her eyes as she listens to the music. "The music. It's so rich and pure."

I could honestly say that I had never met anyone who made me feel like Andrea.

She was like the music. Rich and pure.

"Dance with me," I say, going on impulse.

"What?" she asks, opening her eyes and laughing a little as she looks at me.

"It's beautiful music," I say. "It's the kind of music my grandparents danced to. Come." I hold out a hand. "Let's dance as a tribute to my grandparents."

"Well," she says. "When you put it like that, how can I refuse?"

"You know I'm irresistible," I say, as she puts her hand in mine.

She rolls her eyes, but lets me sweep her out onto the floor in front of the Christmas tree.

Putting one hand on her waist and holding her other hand, I pull her close and we sway to the music.

She fits me perfectly just as I knew she would. And she smells like wildflowers on a spring day.

"Why do you think I heard the music in the attic?" I ask as we gently sway to the music.

"I don't know," she says. "I don't think that's ever happened to anyone before."

"Really? Then we're that special."

The song changes, but we don't.

"You might be," she says. "You're one who heard it."

"I think it's because I was with you."

"That doesn't make any sense," she says.

"Not everything makes sense," I say, twirling her out, then back.

She laughs.

I give her another twirl before pulling her back against me.

Dance moves are fun, but this is where I want her. Right here. Right against me.

Letting her go after this week is over is going to be a problem for me.

But I don't want to think about that.

The week ahead stretches out in front of us. A week full of possibilities and magic.

Andrea lets out a little sigh and I pull her closer to me.

This was going to be my most magical Christmas ever.

And for a guy who doesn't believe in magic, that's saying quite a bit.

Chapter Nineteen

Andrea

CHRISTMAS MUSIC SWIRLS AROUND US AS DANIEL dances me around our little impromptu dance floor on one side of the lounge.

No one pays us any attention and I wouldn't even care if they did.

As far as I'm concerned Daniel and I are the only ones in the universe at the moment.

I feel like I've known him forever and at the same time, everything about him is new.

He gives me butterflies in my stomach and makes my pulse race.

And I don't want to think about what will happen after this week is over and he goes back to Houston.

I know not to get too attached to a pilot. Brothers. Brothers-in-law, Coworkers. They've all taught me just how unwise it is to get attached to pilots.

They — we — have a different kind of lifestyle than most people. It takes a lot of work to keep a relationship going. A special kind of circumstances.

And not typically two pilots together.

In fact, I can't think of a single successful couple consisting of two pilots. Of course, it's not like I know all that many female pilots.

Unless Jackson told him, which I don't think he did, Daniel doesn't even know I'm a pilot.

I wonder what he would think if he did know. Would he still want to hang out with me or would he deem me too much trouble and get out now before we ran the risk of getting too close?

"You're thinking too much," he says.

"How do you know that?" I ask.

"I can *feel* your thoughts racing."

"You can NOT," I say on a little laugh.

"Just relax," he says. "Enjoy the moment."

Easy for him to say. But I take a deep breath and let it out slowly. He's right. I am thinking too much and I do need to relax and enjoy the moment.

I don't do that often enough.

He'd told me that not everything makes sense and he's so right about that.

Arabella insists that Abigail played matchmaker when she first met James.

Was Abigail playing matchmaker again?

James had been the one to see Abigail. To interact with her.

Was Abigail doing the same thing with Daniel?

I'm thinking too much again.

We dance through the whole record until the music ends.

"Do you want a drink?" he asks, leading me to a booth near the record player.

"Sure. Just a sparkling water," I say.

While he gets our drinks, I take the moment to pull out my phone and check my messages.

I have a text from the office.

Office: I know you're on Christmas break, but can you take a quick flight?

I groan and roll my eyes. I know I can't say no.

Me: Where and when?

Office: Just a quick pick up at the Denver airport. They're actually coming to your lodge.

That's unusual. People usually plan their flights to the lodge in advance.

Me: When?

Daniel joins me at the booth, sliding into the seat across from me.

Office: Whenever you can get there. They're waiting at the Denver airport.

Seriously?

I check the time on the original message. It came in an hour ago.

Me: Why the late notice?

Office: Their plans fell through.

Surely there was someone else who could fly them out here.

But if they had someone else to fly them out here, I wouldn't be getting this message.

I glance up as Jackson slides one of the glasses in my direction.

"Everything okay?" he asks.

"It's work," I say. "I need to go in for... about three hours."

"Okay," he says. "I'll just hang out here and when you get back, we can have dinner."

I check the time. A late dinner, but I'm okay with that.

Later I'll think about the way he just assumed I would have dinner with him. He hadn't even asked.

"You sure?" I ask.

"I'm sure. I need to check in with Jackson anyway."

Right. Daniel had come to the lodge with my brother.

Typically I would jump at any chance to fly, but this flight is coming at a most inconvenient time.

I don't want to leave Daniel. Not even to take a flight.

I shake it off.

There is no reason why I should let Daniel keep me from taking a flight.

I could probably even take him with me.

And I would except that I'm not ready to tell him that I'm a pilot just yet.

I worry that once he finds out he'll lose interest.

Like me, he knows just how hard it is to have a relationship with a pilot.

And two pilots together? That's just virtually impossible.

Chapter Twenty

Daniel

ANDREA PUTS ON HER POWDER BLUE COAT AND heads off to do whatever job she needs to do.

I don't even know what kind of work she does and I would assume it has something to do with the lodge, but she says she lives in Denver. Maybe it's a virtual meeting.

I don't ask.

It's quiet in the lounge now without the record playing, so I put the record back on. A lounge needs music.

The Christmas tree sparkles with clear lights and I feel a wave of homesickness wash over me. It's funny. I was okay as long as Andrea was with me, but being by myself makes me feel a little wistful.

As I finish my sparkling water, I decide on my next course of action.

I decide I'm going to finish the job Andrea and I started.

I'm going back for the rest of the records.

Arabella is still behind the front desk.

"Can I borrow the key to the attic?" I ask her. "I'll go back up to see if there are other records."

"Sure." She slides the key across the counter. "Where is Andrea?"

"She said she had to do a job. She'll be back in a couple of hours."

"Are you sure you want to go back into the attic?" she asks. "By yourself."

"I thought I heard some music playing and it kind of freaked Andrea out."

"You're not freaked out by it?"

She doesn't question that I think I heard music. She just wants to know if I'm freaked out by it. Interesting.

"More curious than freaked out."

"You sound like James," she says.

"I'll take that as a compliment." I pocket the keys. "I'll let you know what I find."

"Be careful," she says.

"Always."

Heading toward the stairs, I pass the big four-sided fireplace with people sitting around the warm fire. Maybe I would entice Andrea to sit in front of the fire after dinner.

I walk past the huge live Christmas tree with its clear twinkling lights and tons of ornaments. Big oversized gifts beneath it.

A couple standing in front of it turns and smiles.

The young man holds out his phone. "Would you take our picture?" he asks.

"Sure."

I snap a photo while they smile for the camera.

A romantic destination, Arabella had said. I can definitely see that.

"Thank you so much," the young lady says as I hand the phone back to her boyfriend.

"Enjoy your stay," I say.

They smile and walk off.

I head upstairs and turn right, heading down the hallway toward the attic door.

My hands shake a little as I put the key in the lock.

Silly, I tell myself.

I have no reason whatsoever to be nervous.

It's just Andrea's nervousness rubbing off on me.

It's just an attic. An old attic.

Just because Andrea thinks it's haunted doesn't mean it is. And it certainly doesn't mean I have to be nervous about it.

I'm not afraid of ghosts.

There are very few things I'm afraid of.

A man who flies airplanes can't afford to have a whole lot of anxiety.

Pilots with nervous personalities don't usually make it very long as pilots. They end up doing something else in the field of aviation.

I quietly close the door behind me and walk up the stairs.

The sun has shifted leaving the attic in shadows.

I fumble for the light switch and flip it on.

That's better.

Now I can see what I'm looking for.

I go right back to the box of records, finding it just as I'd left it. I don't know why I thought I'd find it any other way.

Kneeling, I continue my methodical search through the records.

My grandfather would have loved looking through these old records. I even see some I recognize. Some my grandfather owned.

I find three other Christmas records, then begin the process of putting them back in the box where I'd found them.

"You should take that one, too." I nearly drop the record I'm holding as I hear an unfamiliar voice near me.

I look up to see a woman in a white flapper-style dress and a little cap sitting on some of the boxes only half a dozen feet from me.

"You scared me half to death," I say. "How long have you been sitting there?"

"Not long," she says, smiling. "I'm very quiet."

"So I noticed." I glance down at the record in my hands. "This one? Why should I take this one?"

My blood is still racing, but I refuse to be startled by someone else being in the attic. Maybe she'd followed me in or maybe she works here. She could even be one of Andrea and Jackson's many siblings.

"Because it's one of her favorites," the girl says.

"One of who's favorites?" I ask.

"Andrea," she says. "She likes that song about the moon. She likes anything having to do with the moon."

"Is that so?" I turn the record over. Sure enough it has a popular in its day song about the moon.

"I was told to take down Christmas records."

"It won't hurt for you to take that one, too. You can play it for her after Christmas."

She has a good point.

"Okay," I say, sitting back on my heels. "But if you get me into trouble, I'm going to come looking for you."

She grins, showing a little dimple in one cheek.

"You know where to find me."

"Not really," I say. "Nobody lives in an attic."

I set the record aside with the other three I picked out to take down with me and continue my process of repacking the ones that are staying.

"Are you a Flynn?" I ask, looking back up at her. She has to be. How else would she know what songs Andrea likes.

But the girl isn't there anymore.

She's just gone.

I get to my feet and make a complete circle, looking for her.

She's not here and I know it.

I finish my job, slide the box back into place, and take my records with me to the stairs.

At the top of the stairs, I stop and turn around for one last look around. Maybe the girl is a stowaway. Or more technically a runaway.

She's young. Definitely young. Not dressed like a normal young person.

I'll ask about her when I get downstairs.

Maybe Arabella knows why a young lady dressed like someone from last century would be hiding out in the attic.

A little chill runs along my spine, but I push it away.

I'm certain there's a logical explanation.

When I get back to the front desk, Arabella has already left. A young lady named Zoe is there.

"Would you make sure Arabella gets this key?" I ask. "It's to the attic."

"Sure thing," she says.

I consider asking her about the girl I'd talked to in the attic, but I decide against it.

There's a couple coming up to check in and I don't want to start a conversation that's just plain odd.

I'll wait.

There will be plenty of time to ask about the girl later.

Chapter Twenty-One

Andrea

My flight into Denver is uneventful. The best kind of flight.

The middle-aged couple waiting at the airport don't seem the least bit annoyed by the delay. In fact, I can tell they've never flown on a private jet before.

It's rather fun showing them how the seats work and the seat belts and I even talk to them from the cockpit telling them what's below as we fly back to Alpine Falls.

It hadn't taken me long after takeoff that I pretty much forgot why I didn't want to take the flight.

Like every other pilot I know, I live for flying.

It doesn't stop me from thinking about Daniel. That's the thing about flying. It gives a person a lot of time to think.

I needed the flight. I needed the time in the air to get my thoughts sorted out.

My brother brought one of his friends home for Christmas. One of his friends he's never mentioned.

At any rate, this friend, Daniel, and I seem to hit off an instant kind of friendship.

Maybe more than a friendship, even though I'm not so sure Daniel sees it that way.

I'd thought he was going to kiss me, but then he didn't.

I was probably making something out of nothing.

I'd had a dry spell lately when it came to men.

The thing was... I wanted him to kiss me. I wanted him to kiss me very much.

He had been going to. I was certain of it. I wasn't *that* out of touch. I can't help wondering what changed his mind. Maybe he'd heard someone and thought they were coming in our direction. That was possible.

In fact, that was as logical an explanation as any.

After the short flight, I take the airplane in for a landing. My brother's plane is still where it had been when I'd left.

That meant Daniel was still here. I know he's staying the week, so it doesn't make sense that I get butterflies in my stomach just with this simple confirmation that he's still here.

I'm getting a crush on Daniel. The realization comes just as the airplane hits ground effect and as the wheels hit the ground, my stomach drops.

This isn't supposed to happen.

This was supposed to be a relaxing Christmas spent with my family. And now I've gone and gotten a crush on my brother's friend. His friend who lives in Houston.

Not smart. This is so not smart.

I'd told him my secret childhood thought about the snow globes. We'd gone out into the snow together. That first magical snowfall of the Christmas season.

After landing I park the airplane and quickly go through the post flight checklist.

I have to escort my passengers to the lodge. It's quite possible that I'll run into Daniel and since I'm wearing my uniform, he'll know I'm a pilot.

Well. It can't be helped.

I have a job to do.

I get my passengers and their luggage unloaded. Lead them along the dirt path toward the lodge.

It's always interesting to watch people who've never been here before. The way they take pictures of the snowcapped mountains in the distance, clouds hovering just below the peaks. The grove of blue spruce trees that look like undecorated Christmas trees. Maybe I should talk to Arabella about decorating them next year. The chipmunks. They take pictures of the chipmunks.

I take them around to the front door of the lodge and up to the front desk where Zoe will check them in.

"Enjoy your stay," I stay.

Then I head back out the front door. Get home. Change clothes. And maybe, just maybe, I won't run into Daniel and Jackson.

I nearly miss a step as I go in through the back door of the house, not even stopping to take off my coat.

Jackson is standing at the kitchen window drinking a cup of coffee.

"Hey," he says.

"Hey." I stand there like a deer in headlights.

"You had a flight?" he asks. Of course he would have heard the plane come in.

"A pickup in Denver."

"Huh."

I glance around him. "What are you doing?"

"Having coffee. I'm wondering if Daniel got himself lost."

Relief shoots through me. Daniel isn't here then.

"I doubt that," I say.

Jackson narrows his eyes at me. "Weren't you supposed to be his guide?"

"I was. And I showed him around. Then I had to take a flight."

He looks over my shoulder. "He didn't go with you?"

"No. Why would he go with me?" I ask as though it's the craziest thing in the world. Not like it was something I'd thought about and even asked myself.

"I don't know," he says with a little shrug. "You two seemed to hit it off."

"I don't know what you're—" I narrow my eyes at him. "You know that record player you donated to the lodge?"

"Yeah?" He takes a sip of his coffee.

"Arabella needs you to go up into the attic to find some Christmas records."

My brother turned really pale. He looked like he was going to be sick.

"Or not." I honestly hadn't known that Jackson was still that sensitive to going into the attic. We hadn't talked about it in years. I'd just been thinking to distract him from talking about Daniel.

"She can send James," he says.

"She actually sent me," I say. "And Daniel went."

Jackson kicks out a chair and sits down at the breakfast table.

"Did anything happen?"

"Yeah, actually." I sit down across from him and put my arms on the table. "Daniel heard music."

"Music? That's new." His color was coming back at least.

"Have you ever heard of that happening?"

"Not music. No."

"Me either." I get up to make myself a coffee. "What do you think it means?"

"I don't know. So you were there?"

"I was right next to him." I put creamer in the machine.

"And you didn't hear it?"

"Not even a little bit. And he said it was the same music on the record in his hand."

"It's Abigail," he says flatly.

"But why? Why Daniel?"

I take my coffee and sit back down.

"I don't know," he says. "But I have my theory."

"What's your theory?" I ask cautiously sipping my hot coffee.

Jackson runs a hand through his hair.

"I'm not sure you want to hear it," he says.

"Why wouldn't I want to hear it?"

"Don't say I didn't warn you," he says, taking a deep breath and letting it out slowly.

"You might recall that James talked to Abigail, right? Back when he and Arabella first met?"

"Right."

"She didn't talk to Arabella."

"I know."

"Well. Think about it. She's talking to Daniel."

"And not me." I sit back hard against the chair. "But she didn't *talk* to him. He just heard music."

"Maybe you're okay then," he says with no conviction whatsoever in his voice.

"You think it's fate."

No response.

"Do you believe in fate?" I ask him.

"Do you?"

"I don't know. But I have to go change out of my uniform." I stand up and glance over my shoulder. "Just so you know. I didn't tell Daniel I'm a pilot."

"Mind if I ask why?"

It was a valid question. With my newly minted aviation degree to go along with the pilot's license I'd had for years, I wanted everyone to know.

"I have my reasons," I say. "Just do me a favor and don't tell him, okay?"

"He won't hear it from me," he says. "But be careful playing games."

"It's not a game," I say, putting my coffee mug in the dishwasher. "I have a good reason."

I just wasn't ready to tell Daniel and I certainly wasn't going to tell my brother that I sort of like his friend.

I can barely admit it to myself.

Once Daniel finds out I'm a pilot, I can't see him even considering kissing me.

Everyone knows two pilots can't be in a relationship.

It just doesn't work.

Chapter Twenty-Two

Daniel

After my encounter with the girl in the attic, I go down to the lounge to wait for Andrea.

While I'm there, I entertain myself and the guests in the lounge with old Christmas songs on the record player.

I should probably seek out Jackson, but he'll find me when he has time. I figure he has things to do and people to see.

Besides, I'm content to stay here right now. Listen to the vintage music.

Think about Andrea.

Think about my encounter with the girl in the attic.

Had she been a ghost?

I can't just go up to someone and ask them if there's a ghost in the attic. A pretty girl with an adorable smile wearing a white dress from the last century.

But the girl in the attic hadn't looked like a ghost. Or at least not how I imagined a ghost would look like.

Instead, she looked like any person sitting right here in the lounge right now.

My record ends and I get up to put on another one.

Just on impulse I put on the record with the song about the moon that the girl in the attic had recommended. The one she said Andrea likes.

This record doesn't have Christmas songs, but I don't expect anyone to notice or care.

After watching the record spin for a few minutes, just before the song about the moon starts playing, I turn around and there's Andrea. Standing right behind me.

She's wearing jeans and a red sweater. She looks refreshed.

"Hi," she says with a smile.

"Hi. You're back."

"Yes. That's not the record we..." She trails off as the record changes and the song about the moon starts playing.

She looks at me with confusion.

"That's not the record we brought down."

"I know," I say. "Do you like this song?"

She's staring at the record player now, her expression blank.

"It's one of my favorites," she says softly. "How did you know?"

"Someone told me," I say, but she's shaking her head.

"No one could have told you that," she says.

"Why not?" I ask, but I'm truly not sure I want to know.

"Because I've never told anyone."

"Let's sit down," I say, putting a hand on her elbow.

"Good idea."

We sit down across from each other in my booth where she'd already put her coat.

"Do you want something to drink?" I ask.

"A beer," she says, surprising me.

"A beer it is."

I hold up a finger to get the server's attention, but the server is already on her way over with two bottles of beer on a small tray.

"You already ordered," I say after the server drops them off.

She takes a long pull from her bottle.

"Who told you about this song?" she asks.

"That's a long story," I say, sort of wishing now that I hadn't told her.

I'd rather just enjoy the evening. Not stress her out about somebody telling me what one of her favorite songs was.

"I've got some time," she says, wrapping her fingers around her bottle and leaning forward with her elbows on the table.

I'm not getting out of this one.

"After you left, I got the key from Arabella and went back up to the attic."

She takes in sharp breath and leans back.

"You went back."

"I wanted to get the rest of the records."

She nods. "What happened?"

"I was looking through the records and when I got to this one, I looked up. There was a girl sitting on some of the boxes watching me."

"What did she look like?"

"Pretty," I say. "Young. And wearing a dress from the last century. The 1920s, I think. What are they called?"

"Flappers," she says quietly.

"Yes. That's it. A flapper. A white dress and a little white hat on her head. She told me I should bring this record down because it's one of your favorites. Then she was gone. Just gone."

"It was Abigail," Andrea says.

"Abigail? The ghost?"

"It sounds like her. Who else would be up there?"

I'd been asking myself that same question for hours.

I'd said I wasn't afraid of ghosts. I wasn't afraid. Exactly. Maybe the right word was alarmed. I was alarmed.

"No one," Andrea says.

"What does it mean?"

Andrea meets my gaze, but doesn't say anything.

"It has to mean something right?"

"It means something," she says.

Whatever it is, she doesn't seem inclined to tell me what that something is.

Maybe I don't want to know.

The song ends and there's a moment of silence before the next song starts playing.

"Do you want me to put the Christmas music back on?" I ask.

"That would be nice," she says, swallowing hard.

I get up to change the record.

It hadn't been my intent to upset her. Not in the least.

One of these days I was going to learn not to listen to other people... not even ghosts...

Maybe especially ghosts.

Chapter Twenty-Three

Andrea

Sitting in the booth in the lounge, I watch Daniel change the record on the record player.

Hearing the song, one of my favorite oldies about a full moon, had caught me off guard, especially seeing Daniel standing there the moment it started. It was almost like it was orchestrated.

It especially bothered me after talking to my brother about Daniel having an encounter with Abigail.

And now Daniel says he actually *saw* Abigail. He *saw* her. And the way he described her was exactly the way I'd heard her described by the two other people I knew of who had seen her. Both of them were now my brothers-in-law.

I feel almost like my fate is sealed.

I take another sip of my beer.

My emotions are swirling all over the place along with my erratic heart rate.

Daniel had looked so pleased with himself for playing a record he thought I liked.

That was something. It was actually more than something.

After he puts on a new record and comes back to the booth, I smile at him.

Sitting down, he smiles back at me and I see the relief in his eyes.

"So," he says. "I promised you dinner when you got back. Are you hungry?"

"A little. Sure."

"Do you want to stay here or walk into town?"

"I rather like the music," I say, looking into his mesmerizing blue eyes.

"Me too."

We don't have to go anywhere for me to be content. I'm content just sitting here with him.

"Is that you?" I ask, hearing a phone chime with a text.

"I guess it is." He pulls his phone out of his pocket and frowns at it.

"Everything okay?"

"Yeah," he says, putting his phone on silent and slipping it back in his pocket.

It's a girlfriend. I know the signs.

A quick glance and it's back in his pocket. No explanation.

Of course he has a girlfriend. A pilot. A man who looks like him. He definitely has a girlfriend. Or girlfriends.

That explains why he'd stopped himself from kissing me. It was the perfectly plausible explanation.

It's okay. I know how to be a girl pal. Between my brothers and the pilots at college and then at work. I've had tons of guy friends over the years.

"What's good here?" he asks.

"I like the shrimp and bacon sandwich with fries," I say, picking up a menu and opening it, but not reading it.

It's not a date. I may as well eat what I want to.

"Is that what you want?" he asks, looking at me with a bit of confusion.

"Sure," I say, looking over my shoulder to see where our server is. Seeing her behind the bar, I hold up a hand to call her over.

After dinner, I need to get back home and... take a hot bath. It's been a long day. Two flights.

A long hot bath sounds like the perfect way to end the day.

I feel silly now and not a little bit disappointed.

It was Tabitha's fault. And my mother's. They'd been the ones to insist that I show Daniel around. They should checked to see if he had a girlfriend first.

"Everything okay?" Daniel asks.

"Sure. Everything is great." I give him a little forced smile.

The server stops at our table and we place our order.

Not what I had planned, but it's okay. I can deal with it.

Chapter Twenty-Four

Daniel

Andrea is confusing me.

She'd seemed upset about the music. Then she'd seemed okay for a few minutes.

What had happened from one second to the next?

While we wait for our food, she asks me what my family usually does for Christmas, but she seems different. Distant.

"We didn't usually do much," I say. "My parents would often go out to a party on

Christmas Eve."

"They left you at home?"

"When I was young, I stayed with my grandparents. Then when I was a teenager, I started going out with friends."

"That's kind of sad," she says.

"How so?"

"I don't know. It just seems so lonely."

The server drops off our food and we spend the next few minutes eating.

"I had a good childhood," I say. "But I guess it was a lot different compared to your large family."

She shrugs and picks up a French fry.

"When we got older," she says. My sister started a Christmas Eve party. A masquerade ball."

"Here at the lodge?"

"Right here. It's become quite popular. One of the things that attracts people to come to the lodge at Christmas."

"Is everyone invited?" I ask.

"Of course," she says. "Everyone who stays at the lodge on Christmas Eve is actually expected to be there. That includes you."

"Jackson didn't mention it." Fortunately I always have a suit with me. As a pilot I never know where I'm going to be expected to go. I've gone to art galleries. Weddings. All sorts of formal parties.

"He's such a guy," she says. "He's got an extra tux if you need to borrow it."

"Thanks," I say. "But I've got a suit with me."

"Right," she says. "It's a pilot thing."

"It is. You would know, huh?"

Her eyes widen for a moment. Then she looks away.

There's something she isn't telling me. Maybe she's dated

a pilot. Maybe she's dating a pilot right now. We haven't talked about that.

She doesn't act like she's dating anyone. No text messages. No phone calls. And she doesn't have a boyfriend with her. He could, of course, be coming later. For Christmas.

It's not my problem. Not really.

Except that I want it to be.

"Do you want to sit awhile by the big fireplace in the lobby?" I ask after the server takes away our plates.

She looks a little surprised.

"Okay," she says after hesitating a moment. "I can do that."

"You already had plans?" I ask. "I don't want to pull you away from anything."

"Not really," she says. "Nothing that can't wait."

"Okay," I say. "You ready?"

"Sure. I'm gonna stop at the restroom. I'll meet you at the door."

While she's gone, I check my messages.

It's from Sophia.

Sophia: Hey. I talked to your mom. She said you're spending Christmas at someplace called Alpine Falls. Do you want company?

I stare at the phone.

First of all, no. If I'd wanted her company, I would have asked her. Second, according to my memory, we broke up.

The Christmas record gets to the end and turns itself off. Before I can go over and put another one on, a couple of younger people go over and turn on the jukebox to something more modern. I guess they got tired of my old music.

Back to the text from Sophia. This one obviously is not a random text that suddenly showed up after being lost in cyberspace.

She actually talked to my mother in Switzerland? I hadn't told my mother that we had broken up.

I scroll back, looking at my texts. My mother hadn't sent me any messages. She probably thought it was rather strange that Sophia hadn't known where I was. Or maybe she'd just volunteered the information. Maybe she'd just mentioned it, assuming that Sophia knew.

It was possible and it was an honest mistake on my mother's part if that's what happened.

Now the question was what to do about it. How to word my response.

But that's something to worry about later.

I slide my phone back into my pocket. Right now I have an evening to spend with a beautiful, charming girl and I'm not going to tarnish it by worrying about an ex-girlfriend who seems to have somehow forgotten... or not noticed... that we broke up.

Leaning against the door frame, I smile when as Andrea walks back toward me.

She smiles back.

As we walk out into the lobby, side by side, I swear she smells like jet fuel.

Chapter Twenty-Five

Andrea

"I was told I should check out the decorations on the tree," Daniel says.

"Oh?"

We shift our path a little toward the big blue spruce that came from somewhere on our own property.

It wasn't a big deal like the tree chosen for Times Square, but here in our little world, the trees for the lodge and our house were carefully chosen and brought in.

So it was a big deal to us. Just on a smaller scale.

"Yeah. The bartender was telling me that guests bring their own ornaments and leave them."

"They do. I don't know how the tradition got started, but they do," I say.

The Christmas tree in the lodge was decorated with clear lights and it had so many decorations on it, I don't think there was room to fit even one more. But somehow someone always found room.

"There's Mrs. McAtee," I say, leaning close to whisper to Daniel. "Looks like her fellow found her."

Mrs. McAtee, with her dog Scooby, is sitting in front of the fireplace with the gentleman and his dog Astro, who had asked about her earlier.

"They found each other," Daniel says.

"It's adorable," I say. "Mrs. McAtee has been coming here for years. I never thought she'd meet someone here."

"It gives me hope for all of us," he says.

We reach the Christmas tree and take a look at the ornaments.

"If I'd known," Daniel says. "If your brother had told me. I would have brought an ornament from Houston."

"It's okay," I say. "It's not a requirement."

One of the valets wearing the red shirt lodge uniform, obviously a new hire since I haven't seen him before, approaches us. I don't think he knows who I am.

"Good evening," he says. "May I take your photograph?" He nods toward the tree. "It's an Alpine Lodge tradition."

I glance at Daniel. He shrugs.

Maybe Daniel and I look like a couple here on a holiday.

"Okay. Sure."

After I hand the valet my phone, I pose with Daniel in

front of the tree. He puts his arm around me and pulls me against him. He smells like outdoors on a winter day. Like fir trees after a light rain.

"Say cheese," the valet says.

I smile and my heart beats ninety miles an hour.

"Thank you," I tell the valet as he hands my phone back. No point in telling him who I am or even that Daniel and I hardly know each other. That we aren't a couple.

Our heads bent together, Daniel and I scroll through the half a dozen photos the valet took.

I have to admit we look good together. We look like we belong together even. It's a rather strange and intoxicating feeling.

"Will you send me copies of these?" Daniel asks.

"Sure. What's your number?"

I quickly send them off to his phone. He doesn't seem worried that I have his phone number or that he now has photos of us on his phone.

My attempts at keeping my distance from Daniel are failing miserably.

And the worst of it is I don't mind.

I like him.

Even though I know better than to crush on a pilot, I still like him.

I like everything about him.

And right now, I can't think of any reason why I shouldn't. Maybe he has a girlfriend. But maybe he doesn't. Even if he does, he must be open to the possibility of some kind of relationship with me.

Otherwise he wouldn't have so easily given me his number and asked me to share photos of us. A girlfriend would not be happy stumbling across photos of her boyfriend with another girl. With his arm around her, pulling her close against him, to be precise.

I decide right here and now that I'm not going to worry about that.

Not today at any rate. Maybe I'll worry about it tomorrow.

Chapter Twenty-Six

Daniel

ANDREA AND I FIND AN EMPTY CHAIR IN FRONT OF
the fireplace. A popular place this evening.

She sits in the chair and I sit on the fireplace ledge in front
of her with the warm flames to my back. I don't mind the
warmth and I certainly don't mind sitting close enough to
Andrea that our knees brush against each other.

She looks more relaxed now.

It makes me wonder what she has going on. It's quite
possible that whatever it is, it has nothing to do with me.

I've know her less than a day so I can't presume to know
everything about her.

And, I decide as I look into her sparkling green eyes

framed by lush dark lashes, I must have imagined that she smelled like jet fuel.

Sometimes I think the scent just gets into my nose. Imagining smelling jet fuel on her is one of those things that can happen. It hasn't happened before, but there's nothing saying it can't happen now.

I can't explain it and I don't try.

I want to talk more about Abigail, but Andrea had seemed uncomfortable talking about the ghost earlier, so I keep my thoughts to myself. For the moment at any rate.

"How did your work thing go?" I ask.

"Work went okay," she says. "Uneventful."

I laugh. "I can tell you have brothers for pilots."

"Yeah? How's that?"

"Uneventful is pilot speak." I shift as the heat gets warm against my back and my knees brush against Andrea's.

"Pilot speak," she says with a little grin.

"So what do you—?"

"Hey Scooby," Andrea says as Scooby, Mrs. McAtee's comes to put his paws in her lap. "I didn't think you remembered me."

"Of course he remembers you," Mrs. McAtee says from her chair a few feet away, a big smile on her face.

"You have a new friend, don't you?" Andrea asks the dog as she scratches behind his ears and looks over at Astro, the gentleman's dog.

"This is Astro," Mrs. McAtee says with a look at *her* new friend. "And this is Franklin Moore."

"It's a pleasure to meet you," Mr. Moore says.

Scooby leaves Andrea and walks over to me, sniffing my hands. I scratch his head. His collar has jingle bells on his collar. Like we had worn on our shoes at Christmastime in grade school.

"Are you going to introduce your friend?" Mrs. McAtee asks.

"This is Daniel..." Andrea pauses as she realizes she doesn't know my last name.

"Hello Daniel," Mrs. McAtee says. "Are you an airplane pilot like Andrea?

I blink, my mind absorbing her words.

I must have misunderstood.

Although I'm confused, it would be impolite to answer her and I have better manners than that.

"I'm a pilot," I say.

"How nice," Mrs. McAtee says. "Mr. Moore used to be a pilot, too, in the Air Force before he retired. I'm sure you two would have so much to talk about."

"I'm sure," I say.

She'd just thrown that out there and moved right on along. Just like nothing had happened.

Andrea and Mrs. McAtee chat for a few more minutes.

"Well," Mrs. McAtee says. "It's past my bedtime and I don't want to turn into a pumpkin."

"I'll walk you up to your room," Mr. Moore says. "It's past my bedtime, too."

And off they go, two older people and their dogs.

"They're so cute together," Andrea says.

Before I have time to figure out how to ask her about what

Mrs. McAtee has said about her being a pilot, Andrea turns to me.

"You know," she says. "I don't even know your last name."

It seems both of us have been keeping things from each other.

Chapter Twenty-Seven

Andrea

MRS. MCATEE AND HER NEW FRIEND MR. MOORE are adorable together. I watch them as they walk upstairs, their two dogs, seemingly hitting it right off, too.

Two things had come out of my brief conversation with the older couple.

One is that I don't know Daniel's last name. Not really a big deal, but a good distraction from the second thing—the real problem.

Mrs. McAtee had asked Daniel if he was a pilot. *Like me.*

There was no chance that he hadn't heard her. But. He had waited too long to respond.

So... my cover is blown.

Daniel looks at me with a bit of a challenge in his expression.

What I don't understand is why he wouldn't want to tell me his last name.

The most ludicrous thing I can think of is that we're somehow related.

Jackson would have told me that.

It would explain a lot though. It would explain why Abigail had shown herself to him. Maybe he's got Flynn blood.

Daniel shifts to the left. I can only imagine that his back is getting hot.

"My last name is Worthington," he says.

I blink.

"Well. That's interesting. So you know Arabella's husband James."

I straighten my spine. So he'd just pretended not to know my family when all along he's known all of us.

"Distant cousin," he says.

"So you don't know him?"

"I think maybe I met him once. Wouldn't know him if I saw him."

"Actually, you probably would. He's the spitting image of Noah."

"Is that so?" he asks with a little smile.

I nod.

"That's quite the compliment to James."

I smile as I relief floods through me. "I guess it is." It's good to know that he wasn't really hiding anything from me. It just hadn't come up.

My brother Jackson, on the other hand, should have told me this. I'm certain he knows his friend's last name. If nothing else, he would have needed to know for the flight manifest.

"Now," Daniel says. "Is there something you forgot to mention to me?"

"I'm certain there's a lot you don't know about me," I say, biting my bottom lip and tucking a strand of hair behind an ear.

"I'm sure. What's this about you being an airplane pilot?"

"Yes," I say. "I just graduated and I work for Skye Travels in Denver." I say it quickly, getting it out in a rush.

"Congratulations," he says.

"Thank you." I look away. It's okay if he knows. He was going to find out anyway.

He leans closer.

"What are you doing?" I ask with a little nervous laugh.

"I thought I smelled jet fuel on you earlier. I told myself I was imagining it."

"It's hard to miss, isn't it? I was going to tell you," I say.

"I know," he says. "It's okay."

I'm surprised he's being so unconcerned about it. I guess he has no reason to be otherwise.

It wasn't like I'd kept something from him.

I rather think that two people have to know each other for more than a day before not revealing something personal counts.

It takes time, after all, to learn things about people. Still. I'm biting my bottom lip again.

"You didn't want me to know?" he asks.

Daniel is far too perceptive.

"I guess I was a little bit afraid for you to know." I can admit that. Even to him.

"Why?" He seems curiously perplexed. "I think it's great that you're a pilot."

How can I explain my fear to him without sounding presumptuous? When he's made no indication that he wants to date me?

"It's hard for two pilots to be... friends."

"Jackson and I are friends," he says.

It's hard not to roll my eyes at him. He's making this entirely too hard.

"Oh." He leans a little closer. The fire in the fireplace behind him crackles. "What kind of friends?"

Looking into his smiling blue eyes I contemplate what to tell him.

The kind of friend I want to hold hands with.

The kind of friend I want to dance with.

The kind of friend I want to kiss.

Instead, I shrug and don't say anything.

When he holds out his hands, I put mine in his. He turns my hands over. Palm up.

Runs a hand along the lines in my palm.

"What? Are you reading my palm?" I ask.

"I wish I could. I'm trying to imagine these hands with grease on them."

I swallow thickly as his fingertip gliding against my palm sends shivers through me.

"I wear gloves," I say, the words coming out as a whisper.

He grins. "Good to know. I would hate to think otherwise.

He's leaning closer now. The warmth of the fireplace envelops us and the few other people sitting around the over-sized fireplace blend into the background.

As far as I'm concerned, there's no one here but us.

He leans close until our breath mingles.

"This kind of friend?" he asks.

"Yes," I breathe, even though I'm not certain what he's asking me. I know what I *want* him to be asking me.

I want him to be asking me about the kind of friends who kiss.

My eyes flutter closed as he leans closer.

He presses his soft lips against my cheek.

I hold my breath as anticipation rises. I can't remember ever wanting anyone to kiss me on the lips as badly as I want Daniel to kiss me right now.

But instead of kissing me on the lips, he shifts back a little and tucks a strand of hair behind my ear.

"I don't think you being a pilot will affect our friendship," he says.

My eyes flutter open. Instead of seeing smiling blue eyes as I had expected, I see him looking at me with smoldering eyes.

He raises my hand to his lips and presses a kiss against my palm.

I think he might just drive me insane if he doesn't kiss me already.

Chapter Twenty-Eight

Daniel

I'm not sure how much longer I can go without kissing Andrea.

Her cheek. Her palm. Her soft skin lures me to her.

But then I remind myself that I only just met her today.

Today.

I can't discern why that bothers me so much as it does. In our world of fast cars, fast food, instant messaging, why do I feel like I should let my feelings for her simmer like a pot of homemade spaghetti sauce?

Will it make what I feel that much sweeter?

Am I that afraid of what people will think? How they will judge?

"Are you ready to walk back home?" I ask.

"Okay," she says, blinking as though coming out of a daze. "Sure."

We get to our feet and I hold onto her hand, letting go only long enough for us to bundle in our coats. With a glance at me, she pulls her wool cap onto her head.

Smiling, I put my wool cap with the pompom on, too.

"It becomes you," she says.

"It's impossible for me to see that as a good thing."

She just laughs. We walk through the front door, held open by the valet, into the cold night air that feel invigorating for about a minute.

I shiver and pull my coat closer, glad I'm wearing the wool cap after all.

The snow has already stopped, leaving behind the cold that it brought with it.

Our gloved hands clasped together, we enter the forest and head down the path toward the Flynn's house.

Besides the moonlight, the path is lined with cute little solar lights lighting our path.

As we walk beneath the trees, the aspen limbs bare, the blue spruce trees rife with fragrant needles, I contemplate my conversation with Andrea.

She'd been afraid to tell me that she was a pilot. Reading between the lines, she didn't think I would be interested in her romantically if I knew.

A smart man probably wouldn't be. A smart man would know that two pilots would struggle with such a relationship.

Unfortunately, I'm a man already smitten. I don't stand a chance. Cupid's arrow struck me dead center in the heart.

Love at first sight.

I need to talk to Jackson. I need to get his take on the ghost Abigail.

Something about her made Andrea reluctant to talk about it.

Andrea was afraid of the ghost and according to her, Jackson wouldn't even go into the attic.

Somehow I think she has something to do with this, but I don't know what that something is.

We took the path leading to the right toward the house. The path to the left leading to the airport.

"That little Cessna," I asked. "Is that yours?"

"It's one of Mr. Worthington's old airplanes. A loaner."

"He's a good man," I say. "One of the best."

Noah has airplanes housed at various places all over the country and according to rumor, most of them are there as a result of one of his pilots deciding they wanted to stay in a certain location.

There weren't many business owners who would go out of their way like that. In all fairness, Noah profited from each one. His success was enviable by other men in the field of aviation and entrepreneurs all over.

Not only was he successful, but he had the loyalty of his people, myself included.

If Noah would leave airplanes housed all over the country for people who worked for him, who was to say he wouldn't consider a transfer for a similar reason.

I am, of course, getting ahead of myself. I have to get Andrea on board.

"That's what I hear," Andrea says.

"If he hired you, I know you met him," I say. Noah personally hires all his own pilots. At least he did and I haven't heard anything differently. In fact, last week I'd seen him walking toward an airplane with a young man, obviously an applicant.

"I did, but other than that, I haven't had any interaction with him."

"You'll like him," I say.

We reach the back door of her house and step inside the warmth. It carries the lingering scent of fresh baked apple pie.

After we hang our coats on pegs by the door, we walk through the darkened kitchen.

"Looks like everyone's already turned in," I say.

"They're around," Andrea says. "Probably watching television."

"I need to talk to Jackson," I say.

Andrea lifts an eyebrow.

"I haven't seen him since we got here. I can't have him thinking I abandoned him."

"He'll get over it."

We pass the living room where just as Andrea predicted, a movie is playing on the television. I recognize the music as one of those popular movies that is a Christmas movie, but a lot people don't think of it as a Christmas movie.

But Jackson sees me walk by, puts the movie on pause and

flips on the light when I stick my head in the door to the living room.

"Got a minute?" I ask him.

"I'll see you in the morning," Andrea says, giving me a look of resignation.

"Sure," Jackson says. "Come in. Have a seat."

"Good night," I tell her and she turns away. "Wait."

She stops and turns back around, looking at me expectantly.

"Want to have breakfast?" I ask.

She hesitates a moment. Looks uncertain.

"Okay. What time?"

"You tell me."

"Seven."

So she likes to get her day started early.

"I'll meet you down here at seven then."

She gives me a little smile, then whirls around and continues her path toward the stairs to her room.

"Did you have a good day?" Jackson asks me.

"Actually yes." I sit down on the sofa. "But I wanted to ask you about something."

"Andrea?"

"No. Should I?"

"What did you want to ask me about?" He ignores my question.

"I went into the attic at the lodge," I say, pausing for his reaction.

"I heard."

"Well. Then I guess you heard about the music."

"I did." His reaction is shuttered and I can't read it.

"Did you also hear that I talked to the ghost?"

Jackson went pale. "No. How do you know you talked to her?"

"I described her to Andrea." Jackson doesn't say anything. "A young lady. Pretty. Wearing a white flapper dress with a little cap on her head. She seemed to know Andrea. Mentioned her by name."

"What did she say about her?"

"She told me to take one of the records down. The one in my hand. To play it for her. Said it was one of her favorites."

"Is it?"

"She said it was, but that no one could possibly know it."

Jackson sits back. Runs a hand through his hair. Then he lets out a long sigh.

"Andrea doesn't like to talk about it," I say.

"No one does."

"So she's really a ghost?"

"She's really a ghost." It bothers me that he doesn't hesitate. I think that bothers me more than anything else. More than his answer in the affirmative.

"What's the significance?" I ask.

"That she spoke to you?" He shakes his head. "Nothing I can say for certain."

"But you have your theories?"

"I do."

"But... you're not going to tell me."

"Not tonight. Maybe later."

"Got it." I stand up. If he's not going to tell me, then I'm going to get some sleep. "I'll let you get back to your movie."

Jackson picks up the remote, but as I head toward the stairs and my room, I don't hear the television start up again.

Whatever they know about Abigail, it has both brother and sister unsettled. Jackson more so than Andrea.

Chapter Twenty-Nine

Andrea

My bedroom had always been my safe place, at least until I'd left home to go to college. I was lucky and I knew it to have grown up in such a large family and have my own bedroom.

Granted I spent a lot of time downstairs with my family and over at the lodge. But my bedroom was my own little space away from the world.

My bedroom was where I wrote my wildest dreams in my diary. Where I nursed my broken heart back from teenage crushes.

I'd play music and I'd dance to it. Just me and my music.

This is where I played the old songs including the one about the moon. I'd say that someone had overheard my music, but I always wore headphones. The big kind that go over the head and cover the ears. No one could hear what I was playing except for me.

As I get dressed for bed, I let myself dream, just as I had when I'd been a teenager. Except this time I dreamed about Daniel.

There was no dreaming about him asking me to the prom or anything like that.

It was just me imagining undefined possibilities for the week that stretched out ahead of us.

Anything was possible. Mostly I replayed the way he'd kissed my palm. My cheek. The way my lips had begged to feel his against mine.

I didn't understand him.

He seemed like he wanted to kiss me, but for some reason he wouldn't do it.

And yet he made plans with me for in the morning.

Wearing my pajamas, I lay on my back across the bed.

I was like a schoolgirl.

I'd never even dated a pilot. I knew how they were so I'd never had an inclination. Besides, when it came right down to it, I've never considered myself the kind of girl a pilot would want to date.

Pilots dated tall skinny blonde models. I was not tall or blonde. In fact, I was the opposite of the kind of girl pilots were attracted to.

And yet when Daniel looked at me, I felt like the most attractive girl he'd ever seen.

I didn't want to think about that too much. I didn't want to think about how practiced he must be at making girls feel special.

I was good at managing expectations. That's what I need to do. I need to manage my expectations.

Daniel and I can have our week and enjoy it. I didn't need to expect anything after that.

He and my brother would go back to Houston. I hate that. But I'm a pilot. I can deal with it.

The thing I don't understand is Abigail. Why had Abigail appeared to Daniel? She had appeared to Arabella's husband and they both insist that Abigail played matchmaker to get them together.

A ghost playing matchmaker. It was ludicrous. And virtually impossible.

But not *completely* impossible.

Daniel had seen her. Talked to her. She had told him that I liked that old hundred-year-old song about the moon. That it's one of my favorites. Which it is.

If a ghost is playing matchmaker, does that mean she knows something I don't?

If a ghost is playing matchmaker, does that mean that Daniel and I are fated to be together?

That's the best reasoning I have at the moment.

I'm not sure how I feel about that.

But I do know that I'm looking forward to what

tomorrow may bring, especially since it's starting off with a breakfast date with Daniel.

I sigh.

A breakfast date.

That's not a bad way to start off a day.

Not bad at all.

Chapter Thirty

Daniel

I CONSIDER MYSELF TO BE A GENTLEMAN. IT MIGHT be an old-fashioned concept, but I consider myself to be one anyway.

As such when I get to my guest room at the Flynn house, I do the right thing.

The guest room smells freshly cleaned. Maybe someone cleaned it while I was out today. The clean smell is there, but it also smells like Christmas. Vanilla. Blue spruce. Poinsettias.

The Christmas scent is coming from a flower arrangement someone had brought to my room. I don't think it's specifically for me. I think it's just for the room. I'd seen one like downstairs in the middle of the kitchen table.

The arrangement has mostly poinsettias with springs of blue spruce. An unusual and festive arrangements. My mother would like it and if she weren't in Switzerland, I would consider finding out where it came from and order one for her.

It's just as well, though, that's she's in Switzerland because I have a feeling the flower arrangement is made locally.

As such getting it to Houston would be impossible unless I personally delivered it.

I send Sophia a message.

ME: Spotty phone service here.

It's not completely a lie. I did have to turn my phone off and back on to get it straightened out.

ME: I'm a guest here, so it wouldn't be appropriate for you to come.

Yes. Sometimes I'm too nice.

She writes back immediately. She must have been holding her phone.

Sophia: I looked it up. There's an inn I can stay at.

I've never known Sophia to be so persistent. It must have something to do with the season. If she and I had stayed together, this would have been our first Christmas together. I have no baseline for how she is at the holidays.

ME: Not a good idea.

Thought bubbles.

I can *feel* her pouting through the lines. Her pout was one of the things that first attracted me to her. But now, not so much. I send another message before she has time to respond.

ME: Spend Christmas with your family.

Sophia: It won't be the same without you.

I'm going to just have to tell her straight out.

ME: Sophia. We broke up.

Sophia: I know. But that was a mistake. You think so, too, right?

ME: No. It was the right thing for us.

Another thought bubble pout.

Sophia: You're just afraid of commitment.

I groan out loud, put my phone on silent, and set it on the nightstand charger.

I'm not going to engage with her. Not when she's like this.

I've moved on. I've *so* moved on.

Andrea is all I can think about.

We've shared every meal together since we met and I plan to keep that up through the week. After the week is over, well, I'll figure that out when it gets here.

We may not be able to share every meal together, but I have some ideas about how we can stay together as a couple.

I'm getting ahead of myself again, but my Aunt Brianna with her YouTube channel had been the one who'd shared the whole idea of vision boards with me.

I don't have a vision board, but what I took away from that conversation with my cousin was that the way we make things happen is to put them out there in the universe.

Things don't just happen to us randomly.

We either put them out there or else maybe it's fate.

I'm a little confused about how the two work together, but I'm not going to rule anything out right now.

I've met the girl I want to spend the rest of my life. All I have to do now is to make it happen.

Tomorrow. Tomorrow I'm going to have my last first kiss.

I'd waited long enough. Tomorrow I will have waited what I deem to be the requisite twenty-four hours needed to start a relationship.

It's my personal differentiation between a relationship and a one-night stand.

Tomorrow we will move out of the one-night stand zone of time frame into the relationship arena.

I want to make sure she knows I'm in this for the long haul.

I open up the text from Andrea and download the photos of us she'd sent me. We made a good looking couple standing in front of the Christmas tree if I did have to say so myself. That smile of hers is over the top sexy. I've always had a thing for brunettes to start and end it all.

My phone lights up with more texts from Sophia. Without reading them, I turn my phone off.

I'd done the right thing. I'd told her... again... that we broke up.

She'll move on. It might take her a little time, but she'll move on.

They always do.

Chapter Thirty-One

Andrea

THE NEXT MORNING I GET UP AND TAKE A HOT shower before getting dressed. I put on a pair of blue jeans and a sweater. It seems like a good outfit to wear on a breakfast date.

I don't know if Daniel thinks of it as a date, but it meets my definition.

Plans made ahead of time. Check.

With someone I'm attracted to. Check.

I spend extra time on my hair. Check.

Definitely a date.

I head downstairs at six thirty to make myself a cup of coffee and have a few minutes alone before Daniel gets there.

I step into the kitchen to find Daniel already there. Fully dressed and looking freshly showered as indicated by the damp hair at his collar. He's standing in front of the coffee machine waiting for the cup to fill.

"Good morning," he says, handing me the mug of hot coffee. It's frothy and has a hint of peppermint syrup. Just the way I like it.

"Good morning."

"I thought I'd return the favor," he says. "Seems we like the same kind of coffee."

"So it seems," I say, taking a seat while he make a second cup of coffee for himself.

Seeing him here this morning making himself at home in my family's kitchen is unexpectedly... nice.

"So," he says sitting down across from me, a little smile on his lips. "Would you like me to make you breakfast or do you have some place in mind to go? The lodge maybe?"

"Why is it guys can always make breakfast?"

"I didn't know that was a thing. I can make lunch and dinner, too."

"Wait." I look at him sideways. "You cook?"

"I'm a single guy. Of course I cook. Don't you?"

"I can survive."

He puts a second mug beneath the coffee dispenser.

"So? What do you think?"

I give him a little smile.

"I'll take a raincheck on breakfast. We have a cook who would be terribly offended if we didn't eat what she cooked for breakfast."

"I thought I smelled breakfast cooking, but I didn't want to make assumptions."

"No assumptions needed," I say. "It's the real deal."

He turns and leans against the counter in front of the coffee machine. Glances around, seeing that we're the only ones here, and looks back at me with his smiling eyes.

"Are we getting a romantic breakfast for two?" he asks.

His question catches me off guard. I just stare blankly at him for a moment, blinking like a deer in headlights, as my heart races off out of control.

Then I remind myself to breathe.

He's just teasing me. It's not a comment to take seriously.

"It looks like it," I say, giving him a little smile and sitting down at the table.

My heart is still racing, but I can recognize teasing when I hear it. Daniel is teasing me.

Coffee in hand, he pulls out a chair and sits down next to me.

"So how does this work?" he asks

I glance at my watch.

"Let's drink our coffee. Then I'll go see what Cook has for us."

"Sounds like a good plan. What do we have to do today?"

Again, he surprises me. Does he really expect to spend the day with me?

I need to think of something. This is Alpine Falls. There isn't a whole of anything exciting to do.

With Daniel being from Houston, he no doubt requires

something more entertaining than wrapping gifts and playing old records in the lounge.

Chapter Thirty-Two

Daniel

ONE OF THE UNEXPECTED THINGS ABOUT THIS BIG old house is that the kitchen we're sitting in is not actually the kitchen at all. It looks like a kitchen—a small galley kitchen maybe. A counter with a coffee maker. A kitchen sink. Cabinets with glass doors for mugs and glasses.

It even has two small refrigerators. One for water, milk, and juice. Another for wine and beer. And a dishwasher.

But it's not the actual kitchen where meals are prepared. Meals are prepared in an industrial style kitchen through a door *behind* this room where we're sitting at the breakfast table. Andrea explains that this breakfast room is called a keeping room.

The breakfast was delicious. Cook brought out plates of scrambled egg and bacon sandwiches with breakfast potatoes. Fresh squeezed orange juice topped everything off.

Surprisingly no one else joined us. With a family of six children, four of them married, that's very unusual. Apparently Cook makes breakfast for people as they come downstairs looking for it.

The own a helicopter, a private jet, and a lodge in the mountains. I should not be surprised that they have a cook on staff. Probably have a housekeeper and a gardener, too.

According to Andrea, most everybody was already up and out of the house. The rest of them would be down later.

Everyone, it seemed, even though their lives revolved around the lodge in one way or another, did their own thing. It worked for them. Mr. and Mrs. Flynn allowed their adult children complete independence.

It didn't matter to me what Andrea and I did today as long as we did it together.

Jackson may have brought me home to spend Christmas with his family, but that didn't mean spending it specifically with him. In fact, I was spending the week with his family, specifically his sister.

I liked Jackson just fine, but I much prefer his sister to him.

"Unfortunately," Andrea was saying. "There isn't much to do in Alpine Falls."

"It seems to me like there's plenty to do."

"What?" she says with a little laugh.

"Presents to wrap. There's downtown with shopping and

restaurants. And there's always the attic where we can hang out with Abigail."

Andrea snorts, then clears her throat and covers her mouth.

Adorable. She's absolutely adorable.

"I know I missed a few things," I say. "Like playing old records. Dancing in the lounge.

"You're right," she says. "There are a lot of exciting things to do in Alpine Falls."

"We don't have to do much of anything on my account."

"What were you and Jackson planning on doing?"

"We didn't have any plans. I think he just didn't like the idea of me spending the holidays alone."

She nods. "So that had been your plan? To spend Christmas alone?"

"Most likely."

"No girlfriend?"

"Not at the moment," I say. "You?"

"I don't have a girlfriend either," she says, getting up to put our plates on a tray on the counter.

"This conversation just got interesting."

She laughs.

"Or a boyfriend."

"You're funny. I can tell that you and Jackson are related."

"Can you now?" she asks coming back to sit at the table. "How's that?"

"You have the same funny sense of humor."

She laces her fingers together and rests her chin on them.

"It's a pretty day," she says. "We can go for a flight if you want to."

"You'll take me flying?"

"I have a little Cessna."

"I saw it at the air—runway."

"At least you call it a runway," she says. "Tabitha still calls it an airport."

"That's cute."

"She's a sweet girl. Christopher got lucky."

There's only one way to get information. To ask.

"Did she ever see Abigail?" I ask.

"Yes," she says without hesitation. "But as far as I know Abigail never actually talked to her."

"I'm starting to see a pattern."

"There is definitely a pattern."

"Has no one noticed it?" I ask.

"That Abigail plays matchmaker? Of course they have."

I sit back in my chair.

"Do you think she's trying to set us up?" I ask.

"Maybe. But I don't really think it works that way."

"How does it work then?" I ask.

"I don't know."

Either she doesn't know or she isn't at liberty to say. No one likes to talk about Abigail. But I do. I have questions. Maybe I'll seek out James, Arabella's husband. Maybe he'll talk to me.

"Have you seen James this morning?" I ask.

"No. He's on an overnight flight."

Okay. Then I'll have to wait to talk to James. That explains why the lodge's jet wasn't at the runway.

I'm getting the idea that Abigail mostly interacts with those who marry the Flynn siblings.

Jackson is the exception since he is a Flynn. She spoke to Jackson, but he won't talk about it.

Someone will talk to me.

Surely someone who's interacted with her will talk to me.

The problem is even if they do talk to me, I don't think anyone has the answers I'm looking for.

Chapter Thirty-Three

Andrea

"SEAT BELTS."

"Check."

"Door and windows."

"Check."

"Parking break."

"Check."

"You ready?" I ask, turning to look at Daniel. Sunlight reflects off his smoldering blue eyes making them sparkle even more.

"Ready."

My little Cessna seems so small with him sitting in the copilot's seat.

I have no reason to be nervous. Maybe if I tell myself that enough, I'll start to believe it.

We're just going into Glenwood Springs to pick up a few things my family needs, mostly for the lodge. A short flight.

It's not the flight itself that's making me nervous. Flying doesn't make me nervous. Besides, it's a beautiful sunny morning in contrast to yesterday afternoon's snow flurries.

It's sitting this close to Daniel in the little airplane.

We're close enough that our arms touch easily, bumping into each other with the slightest movement.

I taxi out to the end of the runway. Check the two air socks on either side of the runway hanging down against their poles. Make an announcement to the air traffic controller that we're ready for takeoff. Only a formality since there are no other airplanes here.

"My Aunt Madison and Uncle Kade have a tradition they started while they were dating.

Daniel's voice comes through my headphones loud and clear. It seems like an odd time for idle conversation.

"Tell me once we're in the air," I say.

"It won't be relevant once we're in the air," he says.

"Oh." I take my eyes off the instruments and turn to look at him. "What is it?" It must have something to do with flying. A lot of people have little rituals. Like baseball players when they get up to bat. Maybe Daniel has a ritual, but just doesn't want to tell me out right.

"Whenever they fly together," he says. "Before takeoff, they kiss."

"Oh," I say again, biting my lip as I realize I sound like a broken record.

Daniel grins. "Since this is our first flight..."

My heart pounds dangerously. So much for my focus on the flight. It was very bad for him to say this to me.

"And?" I ask.

"We could start a similar tradition."

I swallow and remind myself to breath.

"You say that like we're going to be flying together a lot—"

He leans over and plants his lips on mine.

I forget what I was saying. What I was thinking. Everything except the feel of his lips on mine.

Daniel is very bad.

How am I supposed to fly this airplane when he just swept all logical thoughts right out of my head?

Pulling back, he looks at me with a devilish little smile.

"And just like that, we have a tradition."

"You're incorrigible."

I mentally shake myself. Tuck the kiss aside to think about later. And think about it I will, I have no doubt.

I take a few minutes to get myself together under the guise of checking the instruments again from the top of the checklist.

"I don't think anything has changed in the last few seconds," Daniel points out.

"Right." I continue my purposeful ticking down the checklist.

I take my time because Daniel is wrong.

Everything has changed in the last few seconds.

Chapter Thirty-Four

Daniel

OUR FLIGHT INTO GLENWOOD SPRINGS IS uneventful. The best kind of flight by any judge.

We take one of the loaner cars the airport keeps for pilots who fly in for a few hours and head into town to pick up a few things needed back at the lodge.

Before we flew out, Andrea had sent a group text to everyone in her family asking if they wanted anything.

She got several requests. Apparently this was something normal for a family of pilots and lodge owners.

After two quick stops, she had everything on the list.

We stopped for lunch at a little sandwich shop.

As we sit in the little café near the airport with mostly

other pilots and travelers passing through, it occurs to me that I need to take Andrea on a real date. Maybe we can fly into Denver one evening. Get dressed up and go someplace fancy.

"You seem preoccupied," she says as we finish up lunch.

"I don't mean to," he says. "Just thinking."

"Anything I can help with?"

"Wondering what I can get your family for Christmas. Any ideas?"

"You don't have to get us anything," she says. "But it's a nice thought."

"I'll think of something."

"It's really not necessary."

"What kind of guest shows up without a gift?" I say.

She gives me a funny look, but doesn't answer.

Apparently I'm on my own on this one, but that's okay. I hadn't really been thinking about that, but it had occurred to me in a pinch. It was better than telling her that I wanted to take her on a real date.

I'd ask her about that later. After I had time to plan it out in my head.

Making loose plans is a hazard of being a pilot.

Even though plans can and do change, more often than not, we have to know where we're going. We have to reserve airplanes and file flight plans. Unless it's just jumping in the car and driving someplace (where's the fun in that), we have to know where we're going.

After lunch we head back to the airport, walk around the airplane for a visual check, then climb aboard.

I've been looking forward to the return flight for only one reason. And that reason is our new ritual.

"So tell me," Andrea says as she finishes up the preflight checklist. "This ritual of yours."

"It's actually Aunt Madison and Uncle Kade's ritual."

"Okay. This ritual you stole from your aunt and uncle." She closes her iPad and double checks her seatbelt. "Is this a ritual you do with all your... girlfriends?"

"You know," I say. "I think you're the first girl I've kissed in an airplane."

She rolls her eyes. "Right."

I turn in my seat to face her.

"Wait. How many guys have you kissed in airplanes?"

"None," she says, a little indignantly.

"Okay then," I say. "It's a new experience for both of us."

She nods with a little smile.

"Cleared for takeoff." The flight controller's voice comes through loud and clear.

"But we don't have to continue it," I say. "We can come up with a ritual of our own."

"Like what?" Andrea asks as she makes a final check.

"I don't know. We could shake hands or something."

"Prepare for takeoff," she says.

I have a moment, a very bad moment, in which I don't think we're going to have any kind of ritual whatsoever.

If she just wants to be friends, I can do that. I don't have to be happy about it, but I understand it. Dating a pilot isn't easy. No one ever claimed it was.

But then she turns and looks at me with those mesmer-izing green eyes of hers.

When she leans forward, I meet her halfway and our lips touch hungrily.

It's one of those moments when I know my life has just taken another direction.

A direction that I hadn't planned on going two days ago.

But a pilot knows how to pivot.

And this time my pivot is in a good direction.

I hadn't seen this coming.

I still maintain that my friend Jackson should have warned me that he had a hot sister. At least then I could have been a little better prepared.

Correction. I never in a million years could have been prepared for Andrea Flynn.

Chapter Thirty-Five

Andrea

Why was it no one met me at the airport yesterday when I wanted to show off my new landing skills, but instead three people are waiting for me at the runway today when I'm content to just be with Daniel?

One of the ones waiting is Tabitha. I'm glad she didn't try to come here by herself. She makes me nervous enough as it is just being as pregnant as she is.

She's here with her husband, Christopher, my oldest brother, whose helicopter sits on the helipad, and Jackson.

It's a little bit of an odd combination of people.

But Christopher is here because Tabitha is here and

Jackson probably just got wrangled into bringing the utility hand wagon.

Or maybe Christopher wanted another person to come along with him. I wouldn't fault my oldest brother for being nervous about being out here alone with his very pregnant wife.

I take the Cessna in for a smooth landing.

Then taxi over to park off the runway in one of the designated parking areas.

Daniel and I go through the post-flight checklist together.

"You make a good co-pilot," I tell him, teasingly.

"You make a good pilot," he says.

I look over at him sideways. His face was blank.

"You're not like most pilots," I say.

"How so?"

"You don't have a big ego."

"That's a big statement coming from a girl with pilots for brothers."

"I do have a lot of experience with pilots."

"Have you ever dated a pilot?" he asks as we unhook our seatbelts.

"Never had the inclination."

Our conversation comes to a stop as we climb out of the plane.

"Good flight?" Jackson asks.

"Uneventful," Daniel and I both say at the same time.

"This is scary," Tabitha says.

We all look at her, thinking she must be having some kind of pregnancy issue.

"I'm the only person here who isn't a pilot."

We all laugh with relief.

The guys pull our purchases out of the plane and load everything up in the hand wagon.

"Is that everything?" Christopher asks.

"I think so."

We turn, ready to walk down the path leading to the house.

Christopher stops and looks up at the sky toward the east.

We all stop, too, and follow his gaze.

"It's a chopper," Christopher says.

A chopper coming in to Alpine Falls? Christopher is usually the one who flies in on a chopper.

We all stand there, watching and waiting as the chopper comes closer and closer. It's obviously planning to land here.

Christopher's chopper is sitting on the helipad.

"Are you expecting someone?" I ask him.

"Nothing on the schedule," he says. "But it's almost Christmas, so who knows. People take wild hairs."

The helicopter lands on our runway, loud propellers sending dust in our direction, blowing our hair and clothes.

The door opens and the pilot steps out. Unloads two suitcases, rolling them several feet from the chopper and leaving them, then helps a woman climb out.

They talk for a minute, then the pilot climbs back in and takes off.

The woman, wearing dark sun shades over her eyes, turns and scans our curious faces, her gaze stopping on Daniel.

With a broad smile, she strides toward him and wraps herself around him.

He gives me what looks like a helpless glance, but I turn away before he hugs her back.

I start walking, straight toward the trees.

I can't think. I can't see. I can barely breathe.

Stupid. I'd been stupid. So stupid.

I know better than to fall for a pilot.

I knew Daniel was too good to be true.

Walking without stopping, I turn left at the fork and keep walking until I reach the house.

I don't even stop to take my coat off inside the house. I walk straight upstairs to my room, lock the door, and after tossing my coat over an armchair, throw myself across the bed.

The room mocks me with its festive scent of spruce from the flower arrangement on my dresser.

Lesson learned. This won't happen again.

Pilots are not a dating pool.

My brother's friends are not a dating pool.

Tears stream silently down my cheeks.

I have no one to blame except for myself.

Maybe Abigail. Abigail might have had something to do with it. She was the one who'd sent Daniel down from the attic with an old record with my favorite song on it.

And here I was blaming a ghost for my own stupidity.

This was the worst Christmas ever.

Chapter Thirty-Six

Daniel

I'D KNOWN SOPHIA WAS THE ONE CLIMBING OUT OF the helicopter before she turned to face us.

I don't know how I knew. I just knew. Maybe it was the way she moved or the way she wore her hair.

Or maybe I just knew that her coming here was the worst possible thing that could happen.

She had her arms around me before I even knew it was coming. That, I hadn't seen coming. She was acting like she was supposed to be here. Like we had planned this.

"What are you doing here?" I ask, taking her arms and stepping back from her. I didn't hug her back.

She wasn't supposed to be here.

She smiles again, but it's lopsided now and she looks a little confused.

"I wanted to spend Christmas with you."

"No," I say. "I told you. I'm a guest here."

"It's okay. I booked a room at the lodge."

I look helplessly at Jackson.

He's no help. No expression.

I don't see Andrea. I track along the path leading to the woods. And that's when I see her. Just a glimpse of her powder blue coat as she enters the trees and disappears.

"You're not supposed to be here," I say, looking back at Andrea, panic welling in my gut.

Sophia has no idea just how much trouble she's just created for me.

I'd just told Andrea that I didn't have a girlfriend. And Sophia turns right around and shows up. Throwing herself at me like we're a couple.

Sophia looks to Jackson for help, but he doesn't say a word.

Guess that's better than nothing.

Pals before gals, but he is a gentleman and that means he won't do anything to embarrass her.

"Sophia," I say. "We need to talk."

Taking her by the elbow, I lead her away from the others.

"Why are you here?" I ask. "You know we broke up, right?"

"I know," she says with a little pout. That same pout that had first attracted me to her. Not her fault it doesn't work on me anymore.

"Sophia," I say. "You can't just..." I run a hand through my hair. What's done is done. All I can do now is try to fix it.

"I'm taking you home," I say.

"What? No? Why?"

She truly looks surprised. How did she not understand that we broke up means we don't see each other anymore?

"Sophia," I say. I need to just tell her. "I've started seeing someone else."

"Already? You...? You cheated on me?" Her voice goes up an octave. Maybe two. I hadn't cheated on her, but right now I feel like a heel that she would even think that I had.

"Not cheating. We broke up. Weeks ago."

Turning, she walks off in a huff, walking straight to Jackson.

"I have a reservation at the lodge," she says. "Can you get me a car?"

Jackson looks at me.

I sigh.

This situation is simply going from bad to worse.

Chapter Thirty-Seven

Andrea

I STAY IN MY ROOM FOR AS LONG AS I AS I CAN stand it.

After about an hour, after my tears dry, I spend some time answering email and doing odd things I'd been putting off. Like paying my credit card and finalizing a couple of invoices to be paid for flights I'd taken last week.

I find solace in the mundane. Things that don't take a lot of brain power and even less emotional attention. I even took a nap, something I never do.

It was hunger that drove me out of my room. After a hot shower, I get dressed and bundled up in my coat, gloves, and hat, and walk over to the lodge.

I don't usually walk outside after dark alone, but I have my bear spray in my pocket. Just in case. It works on other animals, too.

The pathway is lit by cute little solar lights that glow in the darkness. I could have walked the distance over to the lodge blindfolded.

The path curves around, follows the riverbank for several yards, then meanders back through the trees, opening out at the lodge gardens.

It's not particularly cold, leaving me not so optimistic about a white Christmas.

Reaching the lodge, I slip in through the back door and head straight toward the lounge for something to eat.

As always, the lounge has a completely different feel from the rest of the lodge. It's typically crowded and noisy. Music spilling out the door. Sounds of animated conversations. Dishes and silverware clinking together.

And there's the movement. Servers scurrying about the tables. Taking orders. Filling orders. Delivering drinks from the bar to the tables.

Tonight it's a little crowded, but I find an empty barstool as far away as possible from the jukebox and the record player my brother had donated. Being near the music where I had danced with Daniel merely drives the dagger of disappointment deeper into my heart.

As I sit down, I scan the room for any signs of Daniel. Not that I expect to see him. He's no doubt doing something with his girlfriend.

I order a shrimp and bacon club sandwich with fries and sip a coke while I wait for it.

Christmas music, of the modern variety, drifts from the juke box.

There's a festive air about the lounge tonight. It's always this way as it gets closer and closer to Christmas.

I'd planned on spending Christmas with Daniel, something that wouldn't even have been a thought in my head three days ago. I wonder if he's going to spend Christmas with us or with his girlfriend.

My money is on the girlfriend. Why would he spend Christmas with us when he could spend it with his girlfriend?

All I can figure is that she wanted to surprise him. He'd definitely been surprised.

He was a smooth one, I'd give him that. He'd kissed me and called it our ritual. One he'd stolen from his aunt and uncle. More than implied something about many flights together in the future.

I'd been charmed.

Stupid.

As stupid as I felt, I wasn't going to beat myself up about it. I'd operated on good faith. My brother hadn't said anything about Daniel having a girlfriend.

He would know. He had to have known.

They were friends.

My sandwich comes out and I eat half of it. Despite my forced bravado, it's hard to have much appetite when my heart was bruised.

I would have words with my brother later about him not

telling me about Daniel's girlfriend. He'd let me believe that Daniel was available.

That wasn't like Jackson.

All I can figure is that Jackson hadn't known.

He hadn't known about Daniel's girlfriend.

That's the only explanation.

After I finish up eating, I wander out to the lobby where it's basically deserted except for those sitting in front of the fireplace. The focal point of the lobby.

It's just a habit, this wandering around the lodge. I probably spent as much time here at the lodge growing up as I spent at our house.

Then there were the jobs. We were all given odd jobs to do growing up. One summer I'd even been required to keep the fire going in the big fireplace. Jackson and I had been assigned that task together. We'd walked around looking like soot covered ragamuffins. Looking back, I think that was the summer I'd decided I was going to move away.

The job I'd liked the most was my last summer here when I'd trained to work the front desk. I'd enjoyed meeting the people. Helping them. Making them feel welcome and valued while they were here.

All the seats around the big four-sided fireplace are taken. Walking around the lobby, giving the fireplace a wide berth, I miss a step.

Daniel and his girlfriend are sitting there, just as Daniel and I had done last night, their heads bent together.

Without her sunglasses and heavy coat, I can see that his

girlfriend is so pretty. I don't see why he wanted to keep her a secret.

She's beautiful. Long flowing brunette hair that settles over her shoulders in loose waves. She's a city girl. Wearing heels, something I would never do here except on a special occasion, and a sparkly black dress that should have looked out of place, but instead it looks great on her.

It would have looked great no matter where she wore it. She could wear it to a football game and look nothing less than adorable.

Swallowing the lump in my throat, I shove my hands deeper in my pockets and keep walking.

Knowing they would be together didn't mean I want to actually *see* them together.

Seeing Daniel with his girlfriend is like a stab in the heart.

One more glance... I couldn't help myself... tells me he isn't smiling. Their conversation appears serious from where I'm looking.

I mentally scold myself. Not my business.

I'm putting him behind me and moving on. It's the intelligent thing to do.

I knew going in how pilots are. I'd just hoped I'd found one who was different.

Buttoning up my coat, I head back outside. It's time for me to go home. Get some sleep. Things will look better tomorrow.

Surely things will look better tomorrow.

I'm here with my family. We'll spend Christmas together,

then I'll head back to Denver and get back to my life, putting my interlude with Daniel behind me.

Definitely the smart thing to do.

Chapter Thirty-Eight

Daniel

CHRISTMAS MUSIC DRIFTS FAINTLY FROM THE lounge. Something a little sad, but modern.

The way the lodge was built is an engineering marvel and I don't think it was even done on purpose.

The lounge/café is loud and boisterous, but the noise barely registers out in the lobby which is mostly as quiet as a library.

The clear twinkling lights from the tall enough to reach the second floor blue spruce Christmas tree draw people like a magnet, second only to the huge four-sided stone fireplace with real logs that crackle and pop behind cast iron screens.

I sit in one of the chairs and Sophia sits in another chair next to me.

After I'd escorted her to the lodge and gotten her settled in, I'd waited for her to come down from her room so we could talk.

First I'd taken her to dinner in the lounge and as bad as it probably was I'd been on edge the whole time hoping that Andrea wouldn't see us.

The thing about Sophia is that I like her. I actually *like* her as a person. Just not as a girlfriend.

She understood that we had broken up. She is actually quite smart. She has a Ph.D. in literature.

From what I could discern, she had quite simply hoped that if I saw her again, I would change my mind and we would get back together.

I hadn't realized just how attached she'd gotten to me.

We hadn't been what I thought of as serious. We hadn't been engaged or anything like that. In fact, we only saw each other about once a week. But. And this is where she seemed to have confused. This had gone on for eight months. And I had taken her home to meet my parents. Oops.

I'd let our relationship go on mostly because it was easy. I didn't like going on random dates with strangers. With Sophia, I always had a date when I needed or wanted one. An added bonus was that my parents were happy to see me with what they called a nice girl. And my dad, being a college professor, had gotten along so well with her. They could talk university life for hours.

They were happy enough with her that she and my mother

talked on the phone and Mother had obviously volunteered my location.

I didn't want to hurt her. I just didn't want to be with her.

I wanted to be with Andrea.

"Sophia," I say. "I'm going to get us something to drink. You wait here and save our seats."

Sophia smiled and agreed.

I'd even tried being blunt with her, but tears had sprung to her eyes and she had looked like a pitiful puppy dog.

I was at a loss as to how to cut her loose without being an ass. But being an ass looked like it was going to be my next course of action.

Coming out of the restroom, I spot Jackson sitting at the bar in the lounge.

"Hey," he says as I slide onto a stool next to his. "How's it going?"

"I'm in hell," I say, running a hand through my hair and massaging the back of my neck.

"So it seems." Jackson takes a swig of his beer. "Want a beer?"

"Do I ever," I glance over my shoulder. "But I told Sophia I'd be right back. Bring us something to drink."

Jackson nods. Doesn't say anything while I order two sparkling waters mixed with orange juice. Skye Mimosa ™, we call it, the name coined from our company Skye Travels.

Deep in thought, Jackson taps his beer bottle.

"Let me talk to her," he says, finally.

"What? Why?"

"Maybe I can help," he says. "If you don't want me to, I understand."

I sit back, blow out a breath. This is a tricky situation. I want to date, maybe more, Jackson's sister. And yet here I am trying to navigate a breakup with Sophia.

Maybe I need to make sure he understands.

"I'm not sure you know this or not," I say. "But I like your sister. Andrea."

"I got that impression."

"You don't have a problem with it?" I ask, watching Jackson carefully. Not what I would do if he does. Wouldn't change how I feel about Andrea. "I have honorable intentions."

"No," he says, an amused smile playing about his lips. "Do you have a problem with me talking to Sophia?"

"No." I watch Jackson through narrowed eyes. Jackson has never said much about Sophia one way or the other. I remember him telling me once that I was lucky.

That's about all I can remember him saying. I hadn't thought much of it at the time.

"What about Andrea?" I ask.

"What about her?" Jackson keeps his gaze blank and straight ahead.

"Do you think she's going to be understanding?"

"I'd give her some time. Let her see you sorted it out. Then do some serious sucking up."

I snort. "And that's your official advice?"

"It's what I've got."

The bartender slides my two Skye Mimosas over to me.

"Okay," I say, sliding them toward Jackson. "You talk to Sophia. I'm going to see if I can find Andrea."

"Wouldn't do that," Jackson says.

"No?"

"Go home. Go to bed. Give Andrea a couple of days. Let me talk to Sophia. Get that straightened out."

"Alright," I say. It's a good a plan as anything I've come up with. Maybe Jackson can sort it out with Sophia. Get her to understand.

Quite honestly, I'm exhausted from dealing with the whole mess.

Whatever happens I know what I want.

Andrea.

Chapter Thirty-Nine

Andrea

Over the next couple of days, I spend a lot of time in my room. I have to take a flight into Denver and wait on my passenger before returning, so that takes most of one day.

The rest of the time when I'm not in my room, I manage to avoid Daniel. I see him from a distance a couple of times, but I change directions to avoid getting close to him. He's always alone when I see him, but still. I don't want to run into him.

The morning of the masked ball, Christmas Eve, I come down late to breakfast. I've been up for two hours, but knowing that Daniel gets up early, I wait to come downstairs just to avoid him.

It's probably cowardly of me to actively avoid him like this, but it's the best I can do at this moment in time.

I'd been swept off my feet and the rug was jerked out from under me so fast I was still reeling.

I'd be okay, but I'd be better after I got home. back to my own apartment... my own world... in Denver.

I purposely sit at the breakfast table with my back to the door, under the pretense of looking outside.

Arabella comes in and takes a mug from the cupboard.

"Hey," she says.

"Hey."

"Did you get your mask for the ball tonight?"

"I have the one I always wear," I say, not even looking at her.

A few minutes later she brings her coffee over and sits next to me.

"What gives?" she asks.

"What's that supposed to mean?"

"It means I haven't seen you lately. What's going on?"

"I've been busy."

"Hmm. I thought you and Daniel were hanging out."

"We were." No sense in lying to Arabella. She knows everything anyway. She's older than me by ten years, so really she's more like a second mother than a sister.

"His girlfriend is here now. So..." I shrug as though that says it all.

She looks at me with a rather perplexed expression which I

choose to ignore. In my mind it's an open and closed explanation.

"Do you want to get dressed and come to the lodge early? Help me make sure everything is ready?"

I'm certain Arabella doesn't need any help. She'd been hosting this masquerade ball since she started it years ago. She has it down to a science.

"I guess so. Are you going to send me back up to the attic?"

"No," she says crossly. "I'm not going to send you back up to the attic."

"Good."

"So. Tomorrow I definitely need help with the scavenger hunt."

I look at her like she's suddenly started to speak a foreign language.

"The what?"

"The scavenger hunt. Surely you heard about it."

"I've heard nothing about it."

"Oh. Well. Tomorrow afternoon we're having a scavenger hunt. At the lodge. With prizes."

"This is the first I've heard about it."

"Okay. Are you going to help me with it?"

"Why? Do you need help?"

"Because people are going to be roaming all around the lodge and we need people to be around."

"Guards."

"Something like that."

"It's not like I have anything else to do," I say.

Sipping her coffee, she studies me from the corner of her eye.

"Have you talked to Daniel?" she asks.

"No," I say too quickly. "Why would I?"

"I don't know," she says. "It just seems like maybe you'd feel better if you talked to him."

"I don't see how I'd feel better," I say crossly, getting up to put my mug in the dishwasher. "I'm going to take a walk."

"Okay. See you at the lodge."

I grumble to myself as I go to the cloak room and put on my coat. Why is Arabella suddenly trying to get into my business anyway?

If I wanted to talk to Daniel, I'd talk to him.

Why would I want to talk to someone who makes my heart ache with just a simple glance?

Chapter Forty

Daniel

LATER THAT EVENING, I'M STANDING WITH JACKSON in the parlor getting ready to walk over to the lodge for the annual Christmas Eve masquerade ball.

It's baffling to me that so many people attend a party on Christmas Eve. My family always had a quiet Christmas Eve just with family.

I actually talked to my parents earlier and they're having the time of their life. Apparently, they too, have made new friends and attended some kind of Christmas Eve party at a castle there in Switzerland.

Times change. People change and do different things.

I don't have a problem with that. It just takes some getting adjusted to.

Oddly enough, I was okay with everything, just about anything, when I was with Andrea.

These past couple of days wandering around by myself were quite depressing, to be honest. But Jackson and Andrea were close and I trust his judgement. So I go against all my instincts and don't seek her out. This is even though I saw her a few times at a distance.

Sophia was still here. I didn't understand that. She had a family and it made sense to me that she'd want to spend Christmas with her family, but maybe that was changing. Maybe people didn't do that as much as they used to.

I'd seen Jackson and her together a few times. I guess he's making progress with her.

"You think Andrea will talk to me tonight?" I ask Jackson.

"I don't know why she wouldn't."

"You might recall," I say adjusting my tie. "That you told me to give her a few days of space."

"Right," Jackson says. "I did, didn't I?" He has a rather funny look on his face.

"How's Sophia?" I ask. It's the first time I've asked him about her. She hasn't texted me or otherwise tried to contact me so I saw that as progress.

"Good," Jackson says. "She'll be there tonight."

He checks his phone and slips it into his jacket pocket.

"That concerns me a little," I say. So far Jackson had been doing a good job of keeping her away from me. Perhaps it was too good to be true that Sophia was going to move on.

"Don't be concerned," Jackson says, clapping me companionably on the upper arm. "Just find Andrea. Talk to her."

"Okay," I say, checking my tie one more time before I put on my borrowed wool overcoat.

I suddenly have a case of the nerves.

I guess I'm worried. Will Andrea talk to me? Or will she walk away like she's been doing?

"Do you have your mask?" Jackson asks.

"Right here." I pat my pocket.

"Go ahead and put it on. He puts his red sequined mask over his eyes.

"Do I look like a mysterious stranger?" he asks with a goofy grin.

"Yes," I say, keeping a straight face.

"You're a good friend, Daniel," he says.

"I know."

"There's something I should probably tell you," Jackson says, all serious now.

"What's—?"

"Let's go," Christopher says, coming through the door with Tabitha in a sequined maternity dress on his arm. "We don't want to be late. We do not want to unleash Arabella's wrath on our heads."

"No." Jackson says. "He's right."

Whatever Jackson was going to tell me is lost into the world of things never spoken as we all head out the door to walk over to the lodge.

Chapter Forty-One

Andrea

ARABELLA IS IN HER ELEMENT.

An seven-piece orchestra warms up on one end of the lobby, happily interrupting the normal quietness of the lodge. Their discordant notes are a music all their own but in a few minutes, they'll be playing Christmas music and that will go on through the evening until Midnight.

Guests are already coming downstairs, wearing their finest. Men wearing black tuxes. The masquerade ball has evolved into a black tie event. I'm not sure how Arabella pulled that off in the little town of Alpine Fall, but she did.

The ladies wear sequined ballgowns, mostly in red or deep forest green. A couple of older ladies wear black gowns.

Everyone has masks, some of them quite elaborate, over their eyes.

Even Zoe, manning the front desk is dressed in a pretty silver dress. She's there with her husband. I can't remember his name.

Arabella knows everyone. She knows every single guest by name. She even knows which room they're in. It's her superpower.

Zoe hangs up the phone, then waves Arabella over. They talk a minute. Then Arabella waves me over.

Carefully walking in heels that I rarely ever wear and my own deep blue sequined gown—I had to be different—I make my way over to the front desk.

"Andrea," Arabella says. "I need you to do us a favor."

"That's what I'm here for," I say.

Arabella looks at me sideways, but otherwise ignores my remark. It was true, after all. She'd asked me to come early so I could help out.

"Mr. and Mrs. Johnson don't have masks."

"Okay," I say, nodding toward the box of masks on the front desk. "I'll pick out two that match and meet them at the bottom of the stairs."

Arabella and Zoe are both shaking their heads.

"They want to make an entrance," Arabella says. "Run the masks up to their room."

"Seriously?"

Arabella gives me one of those looks that only an older sister can get away with.

"Okay," I say. Sure. I can do the stairs in these heels. If I fall, it'll be my sister's fault.

I pull two similar masks, both red, from the box on the front desk and start across the lobby with them.

"Room 201," Zoe says behind me.

Mrs. McAtee is coming down the stairs on Mr. Moore's arm. Even though they're wearing masks, I recognize them immediately. I don't let on, though, that I know them. I just smile and keep walking.

Reaching the top of the stairs, without incident, I turn right down the hallway, incidentally the same direction that leads to the attic.

I shake off my trepidation. All I have to do is drop off the masks and go.

I get to Room 201 and knock on the door. I wait about twenty seconds and then knock again.

A door opens and closes down the hall. I don't turn and look. I was taught the importance of guest privacy.

Seeing no need to stay here all night, I hang the masks on the door knob, leaving them there.

I glance in the direction of the attic and jump with a little yelp.

A young lady stands there, not two feet from me.

Not just any young lady, but a young lady who matches the description of Abigail.

A white flapper dress with a little white hat.

A pretty smile. Dimples.

Just as everyone described.

"Hi Andrea," she says. "I don't mean to frighten you."

"Abigail?"

"Yes," she says. "It's a pleasure to meet you. In person."

"It's nice to meet you, too." The words come out automatically. Words I would say to anyone. Fortunately, they're words that don't require thought.

"I don't have but a moment," she says. "I just wanted to tell you something."

"Okay." No thought involved. I swallow and remember to breathe. She looks so real. So... alive. If I hadn't recognized her, her dress, by the description burned into my brain, I would think she was just another guest.

"It's about Daniel," she says, tilting her head a little to the side, her face turning serious and compassionate. "He told you the truth."

I nod, trying to follow. Trying not to think about her being a ghost.

"Daniel has a kind heart. He likes Sophia and doesn't want to hurt her, but she's not the girl for him."

"That's... good."

"You'll like Sophia." She places a gloved hand on my wrist. "Can you keep a secret?"

"Of course," I say. Touched by a ghost. I stand very still. Breathe in. Breathe out.

"Sophia is going to be your sister." Abigail smiles again.

"What?"

"I have to go now. Remember. Be kind to Daniel. You're going to make lots of rituals together."

My eyes widen. Had Daniel told someone... about our ritual? If he hadn't told anyone, then how could...

Abigail is fading. The feel of her hand on my wrist is gone now and...

I reach for her. Needing something... To know.

But she's gone.

I turn around in a complete circle, but I already know. Abigail is not there.

Abigail is a ghost and she just vanished right in front of me.

Her words echo in my head.

Sophia is going to be your sister.

Be kind to Daniel.

Chapter Forty-Two

Daniel

THE ALPINE LODGE MASQUERADE BALL IS AS elaborate as any party I've been to in Houston or even New York.

As a pilot, guests often invite me along to accompany them to various events like charity functions.

A seven-piece orchestra playing Christmas music in the lobby.

Servers in solid white tuxes walking around with silver platters. Crystal champagne flutes with bubbling wine.

And the guests are all dressed to the nines and dutifully wearing masks over their eyes.

The room smells like a blend of perfumes and colognes. Soft. Tangy. Sweet. A unique blend that will never be replicated.

It's quite a lovely sight, but as soon as I walk into the warmth of the room, I'm already looking at every woman. Searching. Looking for Andrea.

"Have fun," Jackson says. "I'll see you later."

"Wait," I say, putting a hand on Jackson's arm. "How will I ever find her?"

"She's your girl," Jackson says. "You'll find her." Then he walks off, leaving me standing there at the edge of the crowd.

He's right. On both counts. Andrea is my girl. And I will find her.

I skirt the edge of the room instead of walking straight through. I'm thinking she'll be near the front desk. The night is young and she doesn't seem like the kind of girl who parties.

I don't see her at the front desk though. I see Arabella. Even with the mask over her eyes, her purposeful movements are easy to recognize.

But Andrea isn't there so I keep walking.

A girl in white materializes in front of me, stepping out of the crowd. Abigail.

She doesn't say anything, just starts walking, glancing back at me over her shoulder. It's clear that I should follow her.

So I do. I follow her through the crowd. People are starting to dance making it more and more difficult to keep up with Abigail.

But at the edge of the crowd on the other side of the lobby, I lose her.

Frustrated I stand there and look around.

A girl in a sparkling blue dress with a matching mask over her eyes is sitting on a bench. Staring straight ahead.

It takes me a second, maybe half a second, but I recognize her.

Andrea.

My heart soars and my nerves vanish.

She's here and she's alone. It's enough for me to work with.

She looks up and sees me as I walk toward her.

"Do you mind if I join you?" I ask.

"Please," she says, sliding along the bench to give me room to sit. "Have a seat."

I sit next to her.

"You look lovely," I say. "But are you okay? Why are you sitting here by yourself?"

She takes a deep breath and slowly lets it out before she turns to face me.

Beneath the mask, I see her mesmerizing green eyes.

"Where is Sophia?" she asks.

"She's..." Andrea knows Sophia's name. I never told her. Jackson. Jackson would have told her. "I don't know."

She nods and looks away.

"We broke up," I say, truly wanting her to understand.

"When?" she asks softly. I barely hear her over the music and conversations filling the air.

"A couple of weeks ago. Maybe three. Before I came here."

She nods distractedly as though this isn't new information for her.

"Have you seen Jackson?" she asks.

"We walked over together," I say, turning, to find him in the crowd. "He's there. Standing next to Sophia."

Andrea follows my gaze, sees Jackson and Sophia, then turns and looks at me again, searching my gaze for what, I don't know.

"She's a good person?"

I can't tell if that's a question or a statement.

"Yes. I think so."

"Good."

"Are you sure you're okay? You look like you've seen a... ghost."

I see something in her eyes.

"You saw Abigail?" I ask.

"Yes."

I realize then that Andrea is trembling. She's not okay.

I take her hands in mine.

"It's okay," I say, sliding close to her and holding her hands tightly in mine. "I'm right here. I'm not going anywhere."

She leans her cheek against my chest and I rest my chin on the top of her head.

I am mostly definitely not going anywhere.

I don't care who walks through that door and tries to claim to be my girlfriend, I'm not falling for that again.

Pulling her into my arms, I gently rub her back until she stops trembling.

I want to know about her encounter with Abigail, but it'll have to wait.

Everything else will have to wait.

Right now I'm right where I belong and I know everything I need to know.

Chapter Forty-Three

Andrea

I DON'T KNOW HOW LONG DANIEL AND I SAT THERE, his arms around me, my cheek pressed against his chest.

It was long enough for the orchestra to go through half a dozen songs, one blending seamlessly into the next.

As my trembling stops, I realize his shirt is damp beneath my cheek. Crying. I'd been crying and I hadn't even realized it.

I take a deep ragged breath. Maybe I'm crying because I'd not only had a conversation with a ghost, I'd been touched by a ghost.

By mostly, I know in my heart, I'm crying because Daniel is here. Right here.

I'd thought I lost him.

But it was nothing more than a simple misunderstanding.

So silly and yet it had broken my heart.

I'd pulled myself together and I knew I would move on. I had no choice.

But now I didn't have to. I didn't have to move on.

Abigail had all but told me that Daniel and I would be together.

You're going to make lots of rituals together.

That sounded to me like we were going to be together.

"Where have you been?" I ask, lifting my head from his chest and looking into his mesmerizing blue eyes.

"Jackson told me to give you some space. A couple of days."

I glance out at the dance floor. Jackson is there. Still standing next to Sophia. She's wearing a silver dress. The only guest wearing a silver dress and she wears it well.

The look on my brother's face tells me everything. Jackson is in love with her.

"How long has Jackson known Sophia?" I ask.

"He met her the same time I did. About ten months or so ago, I guess."

"I see."

Jackson had known Sophia long enough to fall in love with her. How tortured he must have been seeing one of his best friends with the girl he loved. I wondered if he had fallen in love with her instantly or if it had taken time.

I wondered if he felt the same way for her that I feel for Daniel.

Had it been love at first sight for him?

If it had, I feel for what he must have endured seeing Daniel and Sophia together.

"Dance with me," Daniel says.

"Now?"

He smiles a little.

"It seems like the time and place."

Unlike the lounge in the middle of the day.

"Okay," I say.

We don't talk during the first song as he sweeps me in a waltz around the lobby turned ballroom.

As the second song, a slow song starts, he pulls me close.

"How would you feel about having company in Denver?"

"You want to visit?" I ask, my head nestled against his chest.

"Not that kind of company," he says. "More of the permanent variety."

I jerk my head up, looking into his eyes. He keeps talking.

"I have to talk to Noah Worthington first. To see if he can get on board with it."

Noah. Our boss at Skye Travels.

He'd talk to his boss for me.

You're going to make lots of rituals together.

"I feel okay about company," I say, feeling a smile playing about my lips.

"Good," he says. "Because I have an appointment with him on Monday."

"You made an appointment?" I bite my lip to try unsuccessfully to stop the grin on my face from widening.

"I did. Jackson said to give you some space. He didn't say I couldn't go ahead and make plans."

"You made plans?" I ask.

"I did. Nothing definite. Just a tentative flight plan."

Smiling to myself, I lean my head against his chest again.

He filed a tentative flight plan. Not an actual flight plan. A plan for our lives.

I get that.

I understand it perfectly.

We're both pilots.

And now I understand. The only guy for me had to be a pilot.

I'd avoided getting too attached to anyone. I'd thought it was a cognitive choice.

But it wasn't.

It was my heart waiting for Daniel.

A pilot like me. A man who spoke my language.

My true north.

THE END.

Keep Reading for a Preview of
A Ghost of Christmas Magic...

AUTHOR OF STRANDED IN ALPINE FALLS

KATHRYN KALEIGH

A Ghost of
CHRISTMAS MAGIC

CHRISTMAS IN ALPINE FALLS

A Ghost of Christmas Magic

PREVIEW

Prologue
Jackson Flynn
Twenty Years Ago

"I wonder what this is," my sister Andrea muses standing in front of something about six feet tall with a white sheet covering it.

"I don't know," I say.

She tugs the sheet off of a tall mirror, fading around the edges. It's the kind girls like. My oldest sister Arabella has one hanging on her bathroom door. This one is on a stand though. That's different.

"Cool. But, hey, look what I found. It's an old telescope."

"Don't you have one?" she asks, obviously disinterested. "A new one?"

"Yeah. But look at this." I untie an old scroll from around it. I handle it carefully, but the paper still crumbles around the edges. "Somebody mapped the stars. By hand."

"Let me see," she says, coming to kneel next to me. "I wonder why they did this."

"Maybe they were looking for something."

"Maybe. Look it's dated. 1925."

"That's well over a hundred years ago," I say, lightly touching the faded writing as I flatten it out.

"Bring it down," she says. "Maybe Grandpa knows."

"Maybe." I roll the map back up and, setting it aside, go back to my search. Grandpa had assured me that there were some old matchbox cars up here.

After a minute, I realize Andrea is standing there dancing up and down.

"What's wrong with you?" I ask.

"I have to go pee," she says.

"Go," I say. Girls. Why do they have to be so silly?

She looks at her watch. "We don't have much time before Momma is coming up to get us."

"It won't take you long," I say.

"Okay." She whirls around takes off running across the attic toward the stairs.

"Geez." Standing up, I slide another box over and use my knife to cut the tape holding the lid in place. I'm determined to find those matchbox cars. My best friend Scott is coming over later he'll be so insanely stoked that I have old matchbox cars.

This box looks promising. There's an action figure that's obviously really old. It looks like something my dad would've played with.

Something buzzes near my ear. I swat it away, thinking it must be a mosquito. But it doesn't go away.

It's not a mosquito.

I look up.

It's the mirror. Or something behind it.

Getting up, annoyed, but curious, I walk around the mirror.

There's nothing behind it. No reason for it to be buzzing.

I go back to my box and start pulling things out again.

"This is the best wedding present." An older boy's voice.

I look over my shoulder toward the door to the attic. There's no one there.

I look up at the mirror. It's... glowing.

"You really like it?" A girl's voice.

I get up slowly, the hair on the back of my neck standing up. My heart racing.

I feel a little humming beneath my skin.

I'm not afraid. Nope. Not afraid.

Still. My feet feel like lead as I walk to stand in front of the glowing mirror.

It's not a mirror anymore.

It's a window.

I reach out to touch it, but jerk my hand back as it comes

into focus. Just like a telescope coming into focus. Except I'm not looking up at the stars.

I'm looking into this room. The attic.

It's the same room, except that it's night time.

A young man and a young lady stand in front of the dormer window, illuminated only by moonlight coming in through that window.

"I love it," the boy says. He's older. Maybe eighteen. "I love it, just like I love you."

She smiles as he pulls her into his arms. I try not to cringe as they kiss. But curiosity won't let me look away.

"What are you going to do with it?" she asks. "Husband of mine."

"I'm going to map all the stars for you. Wife of mine."

"You will not," she says, laughing.

"I will. I'll come back up later after it's dark and get started on it."

"You'll really do that?" she asks. "For me."

"For you and only you."

"I love you so much," she says.

"I love you too, Abigail Flynn."

They kiss again, but I don't even think about looking away. I don't move a muscle. I'm afraid if I move they'll see me.

"I got something for you, too," he says after a moment.

"What?" She grins.

The girl is young. And pretty. She's wearing a white dress. A wedding dress. It's straight with fringe around the hem and stops halfway between her knees and her shoes. She's wearing a little white hat over long hair that's pulled back part way beneath it.

He leaves her for a moment and comes right back. "Roses," he says proudly holding up a bouquet of white roses.

"White roses," she says. "My favorite."

"I know my girl," he says.

They put their arms around each other and he picks her up, twirling her around in a circle.

She laughs and he sets her down.

"We should get back," he says. "To the wedding guests."

"Do we have to?" she asks with a little pout.

"Yes. Here." He picks up a basket, puts the roses in them, and sets it over her arm.

"You're the love of my life. You know that, right?" he asks.

"I hope so. Since you married me."

He takes her hand and pulls her along.

The mirror blurs a moment and when it comes back, but I can't see them anymore. They've moved away from my line of sight.

I step forward. I still can't see them, but I can hear them.

"She said no."

Scuffling. I hear scuffling.

"Stop it!" It's the girl screaming at someone. "Leave him alone."

"You know we're meant to be together." It's another man's voice. Older than the husband.

More scuffling.

Then I hear a scream. A heart-wrenching scream that rips all the way through me.

Instinctively I know it was the girl.

Then there's silence.

And the mirror is a mirror again.

A Ghost of Christmas Magic

PREVIEW

Chapter 1
Sophia Miller
December

MY GRANDMOTHER IS WHAT SOME PEOPLE CALL A seer. She knows things.

I'm sitting at the little square breakfast table in front of a window, in my grandmother's two-story cottage, in a suburb just north of Houston. A suburb with lots of pine trees.

A potted poinsettia wrapped in festive red foil sits in the middle of the table and outside blue birds flutter around a little community of half a dozen bird feeders and bird houses attached to a wide cast iron stand. The bird feeders/birdhouses look like New York brownstones with little perches for the birds to sit on. Grandma designed them and Grandpa built them.

Grandma looks about twenty years younger than her age. At sixty, she could easily pass for forty. However, the old gingham apron she's wearing over her pants suit isn't doing much for her.

She and Grandpa moved out here after Grandpa retired to get away from the city. That was ten years ago. Ten years ago there had been nothing around them other than trees. Now the house was in the middle of a neighborhood with a shopping center right around the corner.

Grandpa had passed away six years ago, but in the four years they'd lived here together, they had made it theirs, putting their mark on it. I have fond memories of them puttering around the little house, painting walls, building bird feeders, hanging floating shelves on the living room wall for their cat to climb on.

They'd always rented condos before buying this house and they'd had a blast doing whatever they pleased to their own property. One of those activities was painting an accent wall in the kitchen a deep cardinal red.

Grandma stands at the kitchen counter mixing chocolate chip cookies for some event or another at the community center tonight. She has one of those mixers on a stand, also in a bright red.

"Is that mixer new?" I ask.

"Your uncle sent it to me," she says. "I didn't tell him, of course, but I didn't need it. I can make my cookies the old-

fashioned way. But my kids always want to buy me things."
She makes a helpless motion with her hands.

"It's nice," I say, looking up from my phone.

Speaking of my uncle, my parents are visiting him and his
family in Boston. I chose to stay here to spend Christmas with
my grandmother.

Grandma puts a bowl of cookie dough on the stand and
turns on the mixer. The noise drowns out our conversation for
two minutes.

"You should go to Alpine Falls," Grandma says, not even
turning around, the loud noise of the mixer fading in the air.

"Grandma," I say. "I can't do that."'

I hold my phone up to her, showing her the text message
on my screen.

Daniel: *We broke up.*

Grandma waves it away.

"I don't need to see that. You know how I feel about all
those modern phones."

I lower my phone.

"He's right. We did break up."

Grandma sits down across from me. Clasps her hands on
the table in front of me.

"I read the tea leaves."

If I hadn't known she was serious, I would have laughed.
But I know my Grandma and I know she really did literally
read the tea leaves.

"When?" I ask.

I love my Grandma, but when she does things like that,

she honestly frightens me. She frightens me because I know she takes it seriously.

And not just that, but I've seen it work. When I was in tenth grade, she told me to stay home. To not go on a date with the high school quarterback. It was one of those first dates and I figured she was just nervous because she didn't know him. And he was a football player.

But I hadn't gone.

I hadn't been all that excited about going anyway, so it hadn't taken a lot of persuasion to keep me home.

He'd been in an accident that night. He'd only had minor injuries, but the passenger side had been caved in to the point that anyone sitting in the passenger seat of his truck wouldn't have survived.

Since that time, I'd vowed to listen to everything my grandma told me.

The funny thing about it was that she hadn't told me anything like that since.

Twelve years. Twelve years had passed and Grandma hadn't given me a single major prediction.

Until now.

"This morning," she said. "While you were driving up here."

My stomach dropped. She'd known I was coming and she'd read the tea leaves. Did that count?

"I thought the person had to be present," I say.

She'd tried to teach me once when I was a little girl. I'd paid attention to everything she taught me, but I'd never had the nerve to try tea leaf reading myself. It even had a name. Tasseography.

"You have a very good memory," Grandma says. "I'm impressed."

"I remember a lot of things," I say.

"I know you do. I know you have a Ph.D. in literature." She waves her hand. "But that was a long time ago and you were just a little girl."

"It was a little disconcerting."

"Well," Grandma says. "Let me get these cookies in the oven and we'll make some tea. See what we come up with."

She's not letting this go so I accept that I'm about to have my second lesson in tasseography whether I want it or not.

Ten minutes later Grandma hands me a mug of hot tea and keeps one for herself.

As I sip the hot tea, I scroll back through Daniel's texts.

It doesn't matter what Grandma sees in my tea leaves, I am most definitely not going to Alpine Falls.

I'll stay here and spend Christmas with Grandma just as I had planned.

I will not go to Alpine Falls.

No matter what.

A Ghost of Christmas Magic

PREVIEW

Chapter 2
Sophia
The next morning

GRANDMA WAKES ME EARLY THE NEXT MORNING.

"I made breakfast for you," she says as she breezes past my door.

With a groan, I stumble into the bathroom to wash my face, then go downstairs to eat a breakfast of bacon, eggs, and toast with fresh squeezed orange juice.

"You didn't have to make me breakfast," I tell Grandma.

"I want you to have lots of energy today."

"Why?" I ask her, setting my fork down and looking at her sideways.

She's got that look on her face that tells me she's up to something.

"Today you go to Alpine Falls."

She looks so pleased with herself, I don't have the heart to tell her that's the last place I want to go.

I even texted Daniel again last night after my tea reading episode with Grandma. Got no response.

Still. I slowly shake my head.

"Eat," she says.

I take a bite of bacon, but what had tasted so good just a moment ago, now tastes like sawdust.

"Daniel is staying with a friend," I say.

"No matter. I got you a reservation at the Alpine Lodge," she says.

"It'll be impossible to get a last minute flight."

My protests are feeble and I know it. When Grandma sets her mind on something, there is nothing that can stop her.

"Edward will be here in..." she glances at her watch. "Two hours and twenty minutes."

I gape at her.

"What did you do?"

"Edward is coming to give you a ride." Grandma says it like Edward is coming to give me a ride into Houston. In a car.

My Grandpa's best friend in the world just so happens to have a son who is a helicopter pilot.

"Grandma. I can't."

"Well," she says. "You have to. I already paid him."

I know she didn't pay him. That isn't how it works. She'll get an invoice whenever Edward gets around to sending it.

I take a deep breath. Let it out slowly. Then I finish my breakfast.

Grandma works in the kitchen, humming softly to herself.

Something is terribly wrong with her. I have one last card to play.

"Grandma," I say getting her attention as I hand her my empty plate.

"Yes, Dear?"

"Wouldn't you rather I stay here and spend Christmas with you?"

"I would love for you to spend Christmas with me," she says. "But you're twenty-eight-years-old. The tea leaves never lie. According to the tea leaves it's time for you to get married."

"Grandma. You know I don't believe that. We talked about this last night."

"I know you don't," she says, drying her hands on a towel and putting an arm around me. "But do it for me. Just take a chance and prove me wrong. Edward will bring you home whenever you're ready. All you have to do is call him."

"Fine," I say. "But let it be known that I'm going under protest."

"If nothing else," she says. "Enjoy the cool mountain air. You have a reservation at the lodge until the 26th."

"You should come with me then," I say. "We can enjoy it together."

"Not a chance," she says. "I have to get these cookies to the community center."

"You are awful," I say.

"Yes. Yes. I know. But you'll thank me later. Now. Let's go get you packed up.

"I haven't even had a shower," I say.

"Then you have lots to do, don't you?"

A Ghost of Christmas Magic

PREVIEW

Chapter 3
Sophia

I AM NOW A FIRM BELIEVER THAT A PERSON HAS NOT fully lived until they have flown into the Rocky Mountains in a helicopter.

It's different from anything I've even done and by the time we land, I almost believe in my grandmother's magical thinking.

The snow-capped mountains stand tall and rugged, grazing the clear blue sky.

We fly over the little town of Alpine Falls. It has a main street and a few streets shooting off of it with houses, most of them with smoke wafting from the chimneys. There's an

Amtrak depot. That surprises me. It's out in the middle of nowhere, but looks like some kind of destination town.

The little Alpine Lodge airport is nothing more than a runway. No building whatsoever. Just a couple of air socks on either side of the runway.

There's a helipad, but there's a helicopter sitting right there on it.

Edward, never at a loss as to how to solve problems, lands squarely in the middle of the runway.

"Remember," Edward says. "Call me if you need me to come get you before the 26th.

"I will."

"But I have to head back to Houston now and I have a flight to Atlanta tomorrow."

"Okay. I understand."

'You're on the schedule though for the 26th," he says, doing a quick post flight check before he takes off again.

"Thank you."

"I'll get your luggage, then help you out."

I stare out the window as Edward unloads my luggage.

There are four people standing at the edge of the runway. All looking this way.

An obviously pregnant woman standing close to.... I do a doubletake. It's Jackson Flynn, Daniel's best friend. This tangled web is getting more and more intricate.

When Daniel had told me he was staying with a friend, I hadn't known that friend was Jackson. I tug my gaze away from Jackson.

There's another young lady.

And Daniel.

My heart does summersaults at the sight of him. I can't help it. My grandmother filled my head with all sorts of magical thinking.

You're going to meet the one you're going to marry.

Semantics. She was sending me here to meet someone I'd already met.

Tasseography is not an exact science, something Grandma assures me of when I questioned her about it.

I shouldn't be here, but I am.

Adjusting my sun glasses, I square my shoulders. I'm here so I'm going to make the most of it.

Edward helps me climb down.

"I know you don't really want to be here," he says.

"How do you know that?" I ask.

"Your grandmother told me," he says with a little shrug. "She means well."

"I know she does," I say. "That's why I'm here."

He gives me a quick hug. "You're here. So at least try to enjoy it. I've heard really good things about the Alpine Lodge."

If it's so great, how is it I've never heard of it? Probably because I usually have my head stuck in a book. A girl doesn't get a Ph.D. in literature without reading a lot of books.

Standing on the runway, a few feet from the helicopter, I listen as Edward takes the chopper up and away, leaving me here.

Forcing a smile on my lips, I walk straight to Daniel and

give him a hug. I make it a quick hug because he doesn't hug me back.

"What are you doing here?" he asks, putting his hands on my arms and taking a step back.

I smile again, but it's lopsided now and my resolve is wavering.

"I wanted to spend Christmas with you," I say.

That's what Grandma told me to say. She told me it's very important that I tell him I wanted to spend Christmas with him.

"No," he says. "I told you. I'm a guest here."

I take a deep breath and lift my chin.

"It's okay. I booked a room at the lodge."

Daniel looks helplessly at Jackson.

I try not to look at Jackson. This is more than a little humiliating.

"You're not supposed to be here," Daniel says again, looking over his shoulder at the girl who's walking toward the trees.

This is going from bad to worse

Finally I give in and look to Jackson for help, but he doesn't say a word.

"Sophia," Daniel says. "We need to talk."

Taking me by the elbow, he leads me away from the others.

"Why are you here?" he asks. "You know we broke up, right?"

"I know," I say, my lips forming a little pout. I don't do it on purpose. It's what I do when I try to keep my expression blank.

"Sophia," he says. "You can't just..." Daniel runs a hand through his hair. "I'm taking you home."

"What? No? Why?"

He can't do that.

"Sophia," he says. "I've started seeing someone else."

"Already? You...? You cheated on me?" My voice goes up an octave. Maybe two. I had not expected this.

"Not cheating. We broke up. Weeks ago."

Turning, I walk away from him. He's the last person I want to see right now.

I walk straight to Jackson.

"I have a reservation at the lodge," I say. "Can you get me a car?"

Jackson looks helplessly at Daniel, then nods.

"I'll get you to the lodge," Jackson says. "But it's not far. We walk."

"My luggage." I turn and start back toward the runway to retrieve the two suitcases Edward had left sitting there.

"I'll get them," Jackson says, moving past me and coming right back pulling one suitcase in each hand.

"I can get them," I say, not looking at him. Not looking at anyone. I'm afraid if I look at any of them, the tears will break free from where they prick the backs of my eyelids.

It's not because of Daniel. That's not it at all. It's the humiliation.

"Sophia," Jackson says. "I've got them. Come on. Walk with me."

"Thank you, Jackson," I say, following him along a path

that leads into the trees. The same path that the girl in the powder blue coat had taken moments earlier.

Jackson pauses. Looks around.

"Where's my sister?"

"Is she wearing a blue coat?" I ask.

"Yes." Jackson shifts his gaze back to mine.

He looks like at me with blue eyes that always reminded me of an icy blue. The dark blue has light streaks of green that can only be seen up close.

I blink and look away. Something about Jackson's eyes has always had a visceral effect on me.

One that I try to ignore just as I always did.

A girl's boyfriend's best friend isn't supposed to have that kind of effect on her.

"I think she's just ahead of us. I saw her going this way."

"Oh. Good." He starts walking again. "It's good to see you."

"Thank you." Oddly enough, this was the kindest thing anyone had said to me since I landed.

"We weren't expecting you."

"So I gathered," I say, trying to force a smile. Hoping it doesn't come out upside down.

"I didn't know you were the friend Daniel was staying with. You live around here?"

"Something like that," he says.

We walk a few yards in silence. The only sound coming from the wheels my suitcases make as they roll along the packed dirt path.

We walk through what looks and smells like a grove of blue spruce trees. They would make perfect Christmas trees.

"If we go left here," Jackson says. "We'd end up at my family's house. If we veer to the right, we'll end up at the lodge."

I notice we veer to the right.

"You live on the lodge grounds?" she asks.

"You could say that," Jackson says. "I'll take you there some time if you like."

"Sure," I say. He's just being nice to me because Daniel was so nasty.

It's a bit humiliating that Daniel's nastiness had an audience. They must know about his new girlfriend. That would explain his reaction.

"Thank you for being so kind," I say.

"You don't have to thank me," he says. "You're a guest here."

I don't know what that means so I let it slide by without comment.

We follow the path along a rushing mountain stream, water tumbling noisily over boulders.

Jackson stops. Puts a hand on my arm to bring me to a stop also.

Alarm slams into me.

I'm a city girl. Being out in the wild like this is not something I'm accustomed to.

"Look," he whispers, nodding across toward the other side of the river.

An elk stands there. She twitches her white tail, then bends her long neck low to take a drink from the river.

We stand perfectly still while she drinks.

Then she lifts her head, twitches her ears, and takes off running.

"I guess she saw us," I say.

"Or smelled us," Jackson says.

"She was beautiful."

"Sometimes we'll see a whole herd of them. That's really something to see."

Still following the path, we leave the river and walk through more trees. Maple and aspen trees now with no leaves on their limbs.

The path leaves the trees, opening out to reveal a large lodge made from what looks like huge logs. Obviously old, but well taken care of, it's two stories tall with random balconies and an attic with two dormer windows.

A couple of people, older people, are outside walking their dogs.

"Welcome to Alpine Lodge," Jackson says.

"Wow. It's not what I expected."

"What did you expect?"

"I honestly don't know."

As we walk along the path toward the back doors, I look up.

There's someone standing in one of the dormer windows. A young lady wearing a white dress and hat. She watches us intently, not bothering to hide her interest.

"What's on the third floor?" I ask, glancing over at Jackson.

"Just storage," he says, not looking up. "It's not somewhere you want to go."

"Oh." I look up again, but the girl is no longer there. Just two empty dormer windows.

"Why do you ask?"

"No reason," I say.

We reach the back door and step inside where it's warm and smells like sandwiches, maybe hamburgers, and French fries. Christmas music spills out into the wide hallway.

"If you want something to eat," Jackson says as we pass a little café. "This is what we call the lounge. It's a café by day and a bar by night. Has good food though any time of day. Even breakfast."

Maybe it's because I'm a literature professor, but I notice words. I notice that he said "we call." I wonder what causes him to take ownership of the lodge.

"And this," he says. "is the lobby."

The lobby is large with tall two story ceilings. Right in the center of the lobby is the biggest fireplace I've ever seen. It's designed so that it's open on all four sides. A fire, a real fire, blazes, sending warmth into the lobby in all directions.

About a dozen comfortable armchairs surround the fireplace, a few of them filled with guests, all but one looking at their phones.

"It looks like a good place to read a book," I say.

"That's what they tell me," he says.

I look at him sideways. From what limited time I've spent with Jackson, I don't see him as a man who likes to read.

"There's a gift shop up by the front door," he says. "And here we are at the front desk."

We stop at an oversized front desk with a polished wood countertop.

"This is my sister Arabella," he says. "If you need anything at all, she's the one who can get it for you."

"Hello," Arabella says. "Welcome to Alpine Lodge. You must be Sophia."

"How did you know that?" I ask.

"Arabella knows everything."

"I know," Arabella says. "because you're the last person to check in today. And I heard the helicopter come in. And..." she looks pointedly at her brother. "I have your identification on file." She taps on the keyboard.

"How do you have—?"

"Oops," She says. "I stand corrected. I don't have your identification. May I scan in your ID?"

"Sure." I pull out my driver's license and slide it over.

"Thank you. I have you down staying until the 26th."

"Yes. But I'm sure not sure how long I'm actually going to be staying."

She and Jackson exchange a look and she doesn't ask me why or make any further comment about it.

"Well," she says as she slides a key—an actual cast iron key —over to me. "I hope you enjoy your stay and if you need anything at all, let us know."

"I will. Thank you."

Jackson, still dragging my suitcases, walks with me toward the stairs.

A tall, two-story tall, blue spruce Christmas tree stands next to the stairs. It's covered in Christmas decorations of all kinds. No evident theme or color-scheme.

"This is our famous Christmas tree," Jackson says. "People bring decorations from wherever they're from and leave them on the tree."

"That's nice," I say. "Do a lot of people come here for Christmas?"

"We're always at full capacity. People keep standing reservations year after year."

"I'm surprised I was able to get a room."

"So am I."

"Maybe someone cancelled," I say, not really expecting an explanation.

"It's possible. I'll try to see if I can find out."

"It's okay," I say. "Maybe my grandmother probably pulled some strings."

"Your grandmother knows someone here?"

"I'd say no, but I don't know. She seems to know who to call about anything." Just as she'd called Edward to fly me here at the last minute in his helicopter.

"Sounds like Noah Worthington," he says, easily picking up my suitcases and carrying them up the stairs.

"Your boss at Skye Travels."

"Yes. He can make just about anything happen."

"So I've heard," I say, a little smile playing about my lips.

"How about we just call it fate," Jackson says. "And let it go at that."

"You sound like my grandmother." And her belief in tea leaves.

"She must be a very outstanding woman."

"Ha. She is."

"Maybe I'll meet her one day," Jackson says.

I miss a step, glancing over at him.

"Yes. Maybe."

We turn right at the top of the stairs and walk down a long hallway.

"The lodge didn't look this big from the outside."

"It rambles," he says.

Candles, real candles, burn in sconces on either side of the hallway. There's light overhead, but the candles provide a nice ambiance.

The candles are behind glass globes. And yet... they flicker as we pass. I turn around to see if they're flickering behind us, but they aren't.

Jackson keeps his gaze straight ahead, pulling my suitcases behind him.

By the time we stop at my door, he's quiet.

"Is this it?" I ask.

"Your home for the next few days."

I put the key in the lock and turn it.

Jackson pushes the door open and waits for me to enter.

He follows me inside, bringing my suitcases with him.

The room is decently sized. It has a queen bed covered

with a white fluffy comforter and pillows. A couple of the pillows are Christmas red. One reads "Merry Christmas" and the other reads "Alpine Lodge."

A poinsettia with blue spruce foliage added in sits on the little desk, giving the room a pleasant outdoor fragrance.

A wardrobe stands against one wall and one wall is taken up by the big window, the curtains wide open.

I walk straight to the window, looking out toward the tall mountains, peaks covered with fluffy white clouds.

Jackson follows me and follows my gaze.

"It's snowing in the high country," he says.

I turn and look at him.

"The high country? Alpine Falls is at eight thousand feet in elevation."

"Closer to nine," he says. "But the highest peaks come in at over eleven thousand, making them definitely the high country."

"Maybe we'll have a white Christmas," I say.

"If we're lucky."

"Do you usually?" I ask. "Have a white Christmas?"

"Usually. But not always." His phone chimes with a message.

"Everything okay?"

"Daniel wants to talk to you. When you're ready."

I sit down on the desk chair.

"I guess I owe you an explanation."

"You don't owe me anything," he says. "And you don't have to talk to him if you don't want to."

Jackson sits on the edge of the bed, obviously thinking nothing of it.

"I feel like I should," I say. Maybe. I can only imagine what he must think of me just showing up like this.

"Do you want to talk about it? If you do, I'll listen."

I look at him sideways.

"Again." He holds up his hands. "You don't have to tell me anything unless you want to."

"I'm not even sure what's happening."

"Daniel thought you broke up," he says.

"He would be right."

"You should know he's sort of seeing my sister."

I look up, startled.

"The girl at the airport."

"Yep."

"Oh no." I lower my head. "She must think the worst."

"I'm sure she does."

I look at Jackson, feeling at a loss.

"What do I do?"

"Nothing. He'll work it out. They'll work it out."

"I have to apologize to him."

"It sounds like it was all a misunderstanding."

"How did you get to be so kind?"

"I've always been kind," he says. "You just never noticed."

Smiling to myself, I look away.

He's wrong about that. I did notice. I'd noticed Jackson's kindness from the first time we'd met.

I'd met both Jackson and Daniel at a charity function last

February. It wasn't the kind of thing I normally attended, but being part of a university committee on literacy had somehow gotten me there. It had been my first black tie charity event and so far my last. My grandmother sometimes attended charity events, but I'd never gone with her.

The three of us had been seated at the same table. To be honest, I'd noticed Jackson first. Daniel, though, had made the first move and Jackson had stepped aside.

I'd often wondered what would have happened if Jackson hadn't stepped aside or if Jackson had been the one to make the first move.

But I never let myself think too much about it. Not when being Daniel's girlfriend meant occasionally hanging out with Jackson.

I wasn't that kind of girl. I was a one guy kind of girl. That's why it was so hard for me when Daniel wanted to break up.

I think I'd known we weren't meant to be together. I can't say when I first realized it, but I'd known it for some time.

It was one of those relationships that was easy. Between his flights and my busy university schedule, we didn't see each other during the week. Just on the weekends and sometimes not even then.

I rather liked it that he didn't require a lot of attention.

I rarely had the energy or the time to put into a relationship. But the longer we dated, the more I started thinking of us as a couple. I'd met his family and he'd met mine. It was just a natural progression.

Things like that kept adding up and then my grandmother did that thing with the tea leaves.

Keep Reading A Ghost of Christmas Magic...

ALPINE FALLS

A Storm
A Spell.
A Step Back in Time.

INTO THE MIST
TIME TRAVEL SERIES

A new boss.
A fake girlfriend.
A secret identity.
What could possibly go wrong?

What would you do if the very system you
believed in, worked for, even lived for,
turned against you?

DON'T MISS ANY OF THESE BESTSELLERS

www.kathrynkaleigh.com

DON'T MISS ANY OF THE SILVER PINES SECOND CHANCES SERIES:

www.kathrynkaleigh.com

AUTHOR OF BORROWED UNTIL MONDAY

KATHRYN KALEIGH

Begin

AGAIN

THE WORTHINGTONS
UNBREAK MY HEART SERIES

No matter how many years passed...
They never forgot...
And their love never dimmed.

A ghostly presence...
A rip in time that never healed...
An impossible romance...

Sign up for my NEWSLETTER at https://BookHip.com/ DJJBALP to get all my romance releases, sales, Kickstarter announcements, and a **FREE** romance, SEALED WITH A KISS

www.ingramcontent.com/pod-product-compliance
Lightning Source LLC
Chambersburg PA
CBHW020544020726
47494CB00006B/1905